UNDERCOVER
LATINA

UNDERCOVER LATINA

Aya de León

CANDLEWICK PRESS

Copyright © 2022 by Aya de León

First edition 2022

Library of Congress Catalog Card Number 2021953500
ISBN 978-1-5362-2374-3

22 23 24 25 26 27 LBM 10 9 8 7 6 5 4 3 2 1

Printed in Melrose Park, IL, USA

This book was typeset in Warnock Pro.

Candlewick Press
99 Dover Street
Somerville, Massachusetts 02144

www.candlewick.com

A JUNIOR LIBRARY GUILD SELECTION

For Mami

She wished to find out about this hazardous
business of "passing," this breaking away from all
that was familiar and friendly to take one's chance
in another environment, not entirely strange,
perhaps, but certainly not entirely friendly.
—Nella Larsen, *Passing*

ONE

A **grown man is no match** for a teenage girl on a skateboard. Even if he's wearing sneakers and athletic gear. We called this guy El Rubio, because of his pale blond hair, and I was supposed to grab the briefcase from him. Then I'd skate the two blocks from the hotel lobby to where my parents were waiting with the car running, and we'd get away clean.

El Rubio was suspicious of adults, so Mami, Papi, and the other grown-ups were out of the question for this mission. My brother was only ten, so he would attract too much attention; El Rubio would expect parents somewhere nearby. Besides, his legs were too short to outrun a grown man. But I'm fourteen: long-legged and old enough to be in the lobby by myself. Besides, teenage girls are rarely seen as threats.

I flipped through the brochures in the bright hotel

lobby. I was wearing long shorts and a touristy Puerto Rico T-shirt, as though my own mother wasn't Puerto Rican. My curly hair was pulled back in a pony-tail and I chewed gum. I had my earbuds in like I was listening to music, but really it was Mami's voice. "The housekeeper says he's on his way down."

I reread the brochure for waterskiing. My back was to El Rubio when he exited the elevator. His gaze moved past me and landed on the young man sweep-ing the marble floor: Hector, a member of our team.

Mami and Papi were letting me take an active role on a mission, but not without a chaperone.

El Rubio walked to the reception desk and asked the clerk to get his briefcase from the safe. I strolled to the other end of the desk, brochure in my hand. El Rubio checked on Hector from time to time. Hector kept sweeping.

The clerk came back with the briefcase, and that's when I struck. I leaped forward and grabbed the case just as the clerk was handing it over, and then I raced out through the lobby door.

"She's got the case," Hector's voice rang out in my headphones. "Made it out clean."

I jumped on my skateboard and tore down the hotel driveway. I had nearly gotten to the street when El Rubio came running out after me.

He was way behind me, but an unexpected obstacle appeared. Two men in business suits, overdressed for the muggy San Juan morning, happened to be getting out of a dark vehicle on the sidewalk in my path. They were clearly expecting to go from air-conditioned cars to air-conditioned rooms.

"Stop her!" El Rubio yelled to them.

They stood up outside the car and cut me off.

These guys were with El Rubio? I skidded to a stop on the skateboard.

Suits and all, the two guys came running toward me.

I did an about-face and kicked hard to get the board speeding fast in the other direction. I'd have to circle back to meet my parents.

But there was a problem. This new terrain turned from smooth paved roads to the oversize blue cobblestones of Old San Juan. On the uneven ground, I wobbled and almost fell.

¡Carajo! I jumped off the skateboard and snatched it up. Now I had the board in one hand and the briefcase in the other. Instead of being a swift teen girl, I was an encumbered teen girl. With both hands full, I couldn't tap the microphone to call in my location to my parents—at least not while I was running. Hector said I had gotten out clean, but had I? Should I drop the skateboard? No, maybe I'd need it to get away. The men were half a block behind me. My parents were three blocks in the other direction.

I rushed down the street looking frantically at the bright storefronts for one I could run into. It was early on a Saturday morning—nothing was open. I passed swim boutiques, souvenir shops, a tattoo parlor, and a bar. The men were gaining. I needed to ditch the board.

I glanced over my shoulder and saw that El Rubio, with his sneakers, had pulled ahead of the other two. By the time I hit the next corner, he was only a car's length behind me.

I cut left. Wasn't there a restaurant just down the block? Didn't they serve breakfast? They'd have to be open by now. At least, the back door would be open for staff to enter. I prayed it would be as I raced down the alley behind the stores.

El Rubio was getting closer. I didn't dare turn around to see how close. On cobblestones, it was too easy to trip. But I could hear his footfalls behind me.

Up ahead, I saw the metal gate to the restaurant's back door was open. Yes! But El Rubio was too close. I could hear his breathing. When I slowed to enter the door, he would definitely catch me.

I felt his hand brush my ponytail. He'd tried to grab it but hadn't quite gotten ahold. Another few steps and he'd catch me.

A few strides before the kitchen door, I flung the skateboard at him, wheels down. As I slowed a fraction to run inside the restaurant, I saw El Rubio step on the board and go flying. The closer of the two men in suits crashed into him.

I yanked open the door as the third man stumbled into the pileup.

A middle-aged woman stood at an island in the center of a narrow kitchen making pastries.

"¡Señora!" I rasped in Spanish through heaving lungs. "There's a man chasing me. Can you help?"

She looked from my eyes to the briefcase in my hand. She nodded once, quickly, and motioned for me to duck down and hide on the far side of the kitchen island.

My heart was pounding. I had to struggle to breathe quietly after all that running. I heard the footfalls of a man's dress shoes come through the door.

I couldn't see him, but I saw the woman. She was looking into the restaurant, as though I had just run past her.

"Hey!" she yelled after absolutely no one. "You can't go in there. We're not open yet."

The suit guy thundered into the empty restaurant, just as El Rubio and the other man came in. El Rubio was limping, but the two of them rushed after the first suit.

I whispered "gracias" as I ran out the back door. My skateboard had rolled too far out of reach, so I didn't bother to grab it. I ran down the alley.

With my free hand, I hit my phone's mic. "I've got it!" I said. "But I hit a snag and I'm lost in Old San Juan. Guide me in!"

I heard a few clicks as I ran to the end of the block.

"We've got your location," Mami said.

"Turn left," Papi said. I heard the sound of the car's motor accelerating.

There was a shout behind me, and a backward glance confirmed that the men in suits were in pursuit.

I ran to the end of the block. The team's nondescript rental car screeched to a halt.

I opened the door and heard a shot ring out. One of the men in suits had a handgun raised and was running toward us.

I jumped into the car. The other man was reaching into his shoulder holster. El Rubio came limping out from the alley behind them.

Before I had even closed the door, Mami was gunning the motor.

"Andréa," Mami said. "What the hell happened?"

"Two guys," I said. "They cut me off. I couldn't skate—" I could barely get the words out I was so winded.

"She's okay, querida," Papi said. "Let her catch her breath."

"Put on your seat belt!" Mami snapped.

I leaned back and buckled in, sinking against the soft upholstery.

"Where's your skateboard?" my younger brother, Carlos, asked.

"I—I used it as a weapon," I said.

"You hit him with it?" he asked, eyes wide.

"I tripped him," I said.

He laughed with delight.

We stopped laughing as we heard another shot. A dark sedan was on our tail.

"Get down!" Papi yelled. My brother and I dove toward each other in the back seat. Papi ducked down in front. Mami hunched down as she drove, mashing down her wild, dark curls into the upholstery of the front seat.

I heard Papi's muffled voice as he called our handler.

"Jerrold," he said. "We've got the briefcase, but we're being pursued."

"I thought El Rubio was working alone," Mami said accusingly.

"Later," Papi hissed. Then to Jerrold: "Get us out of here."

"You're in the subcompact, right?" Jerrold asked.

"Yes," Papi said. "Do you have our location?"

"I do," Jerrold said. "Hang a left at this corner!"

Mami swung left, and we all leaned hard with the momentum.

"Bárbara," Jerrold said. "Halfway down this block, there's a narrow alley. It's one-way, and you'll be going against the traffic. If no one is coming, take a sharp right. In the middle of that block, turn left down another alley, and you'll be going in the proper direction. Your pursuers will likely get cut off."

Mami slowed a little, and we looked down the block. A blue car had just turned into the alley from the far end, but there was time for us to get through. Perfect.

Mami cut a hard right, and we lurched in the other direction. The blue car leaned on the horn. Mami gunned it toward the corner in the middle of the block.

Behind us the sedan turned into the alley with a screech of tires.

"Which way?" Mami asked Jerrold.

"Left!"

Mami swerved left. We lurched again, just missing the oncoming car.

Carlos and I weren't ducking now. We watched out the back window for the sedan. The blue car came down past the alley, horn still blaring, brakes shrieking. We heard a crash, but we couldn't see anything.

And then the tail of the blue car came into view. Then the middle. Then the smashed front. The sedan had crashed into the blue car and was pushing it backward across the mouth of the alley.

The sedan backed up, crumpled bumper and all, and turned down the alley after us.

"They're still in pursuit," Papi said.

"Shoot," Jerrold said. "Okay. What are they driving?"

"Dark sedan," Papi said. "K-car type."

"Great," Jerrold said. "Keep going straight. You'll be able to lose them in a block."

A shot rang out.

"They're shooting?" Jerrold asked.

"Yes!" Mami said. "Jerrold, you promised the guy wouldn't be armed—"

"Not the time, querida," Papi said.

"Agreed," Jerrold said. "At the next corner, you'll be able to lose them."

"It's blocked off," Papi said. At the corner, a stubby metal pole stuck up in the middle of the roadway.

"Your car will fit through," Jerrold said.

"I don't think so," Mami said.

"Not without a scratch," Jerrold said. "But you'll fit if you go up on the sidewalk. Slow a bit to make sure. Go through on the left side."

We were barreling toward the pole, the buildings on either side a blur.

"Get down, kids!" Mami yelled.

Carlos and I didn't see the car squeeze through the space with the metal pole, but we heard it: the scrape of metal on metal and against the cement of the building.

The door crunched. My window cracked, the glass turning to crumbled squares that looked like sugar candy.

We heard the second crunch of metal on metal when the sedan tried to follow.

I brushed crumbs of glass out of my hair.

"We made it!" Carlos said. "The other guys crashed into the pole."

"Jerrold," Mami said. "You promised us this would be an easy mission!"

"I'm sorry, Bárbara," he said. "Our intel said he was working alone."

We were all sitting up now, watching out the back of the car as tourists and workers gaped at the crashed vehicle behind us.

"When I agreed to bring my family into this life, I had one rule," Mami said. I knew this tone of voice. She was getting ready to go on a rant.

"Bárbara," Papi said. "We all know you're upset. But can we please debrief the details later?"

Mami took a breath. "I'd like to debrief as soon as you can extract us," she said through clenched teeth.

"The team's on their way," Jerrold said.

Twenty minutes later, we were in a helicopter, flying over San Juan to the airport. I still had the briefcase in my hand.

In our family, there's a before and an after. Carlos is too young to remember. But when I was five, Mami and Papi sat me down.

They told me we'd be leaving Washington, DC, where we'd always lived, and moving around for a while, for Papi's job. I'd be homeschooled. Which was great! I was not a big fan of school. The only bad part was that I missed my best friend, Lucía. At first, we would video call. But what do kindergartners have to talk about? We couldn't play together on video. Soon enough that dropped off. Over the next two years, my family lived in six cities.

It's hard to make friends when you move a lot. It's almost impossible when you're also homeschooled. I was always out of sync with kids my age. When we finally settled in Los Angeles, I was used to being with just my family. Mami taught me and Carlos. There were neighborhood children I played with sometimes. We'd get invited to birthday parties or the occasional cook-out, but mostly we kept to ourselves. Books became my best friends.

Papi worked a lot, often traveling, but when he was home, he helped teach us. When Carlos was five and I was nine, Mami started working, too. Our parents took turns going out of town.

It was like living in two different families. Mami was the one you wanted on duty if you were bored. She came up with a million fun things to do. She did amazing crafts or helped us put on elaborate performances. Papi was the one you wanted to be on duty if you did something to get in trouble. Like if you were going to break the rules and skateboard in the house? And break the lamp? Do that while Papi was home. You did not want to get on the wrong side of Mami's temper.

Then, two years ago, they sat me *and* Carlos down. They said the whole family was going to start traveling together. For six months, we hung out in hotels in different countries. Mostly, it was like being on vacation, but occasionally, Mami or Papi would go out alone.

Carlos didn't ask questions. He was just happy to be going places that had a pool. But I got curious. When Mami and Papi spoke to each other, they sometimes referred to their work as "the Factory." What did the Factory make? What did Mami and Papi do for the Factory? How come we had never gone to any actual factory? The answers I got were vague—about reviewing the quality of different hotels and then writing reports about them. Seriously? Is that even a real job? And why would that make them so tense sometimes? It didn't add up.

One night, we were in a hotel room in Houston, Texas. Papi and Carlos were snoring. I heard Mami get out of bed. The nightstand clock said it was almost midnight. Where was she going?

The moment she closed the door, I slipped out of bed and pulled on my jeans. I was a few steps behind her.

"Mami, wait!" I said, stumbling down the hall toward the elevator.

"Andréa!" she hissed. "Go back to bed."

"No way," I said. "You don't need to go out at midnight to review the quality of this hotel. What's going on?"

The elevator dinged.

"Go back to the room," she said.

"No," I said. "I'm twelve. I'm not a baby like Carlos. What's going on in our family?"

Mami looked at her watch. Her eyes flitted to the closed door of our room.

"Fine," she said. "You need to do exactly what I tell you."

She pulled me into the elevator and barked quick instructions. I stood there and nodded. What had I just done? Did I really want to be involved in whatever this was?

Per her instructions, I stormed off the elevator and past the front desk yelling, "You treat me like a baby! You never let me do anything!" I tore through the lobby and bumped into a tall man, knocking him over. Mami put out a hand to help him up.

She chased me out the door and into the muggy Texas night.

I wasn't sure where to go. Were we still acting?

"Come back here, Michelle!" she yelled after me.

Michelle? Was I Michelle?

I kept storming away. She caught up to me and grabbed my arm. She spun me and pulled me toward her.

"Act like you're upset," she murmured. "Pretend you're crying."

"I just can't take it anymore!" I wailed into her chest.

"Oh, honey," she said. "I'm so sorry. About everything."

"What's happening?" I asked in a quiet voice. "You're an FBI agent or something?"

"Keep pretending to cry," she said. "Not FBI. We work for an independent organization."

"There's no factory?" I asked.

"The Factory *is* the organization," she said. "Now pretend we've had a breakthrough . . . Michelle."

I threw my arms around her. It really was a breakthrough. She trusted me? Enough to tell me the truth? When I hugged her, I meant it.

Back in our hotel bathroom, we sat on the tile floor, and she showed me a microchip she'd gotten from the tall man in the lobby.

"What's on it?" I asked.

"No idea," she said.

"How do you know it's not something . . . bad?" I asked.

"I trust the Factory," she said.

"And what's the Factory?"

"It's an international intelligence organization that serves people of color."

"When you and Papi went out of town, it was to spy?"

She nodded.

"You started working for them when we moved to LA?"

She shook her head. "We worked desk jobs for them in DC," she said. "I took time off when I had you and Carlos. But then the political situation . . . well . . . they needed us again. Since spies usually work alone, a person traveling with a family is . . . kind of . . . hiding in plain sight."

"We're part of your cover?" I asked.

"You were," she said. "But now that you know, you're a spy, too. And you can't tell anyone."

I was homeschooled. Who was I gonna tell?

Within six months, she and Papi brought Carlos in on it, and we were a family of spies.

Two

In the San Juan airport, Mami's tirade to Jerrold was in murmured tones, but I knew that rage. She had the phone in her pocket and earbuds in her ears. She paced across the carpet, her hands speaking louder than her voice.

Maybe in Denver or Charlotte, this would have drawn attention. But in San Juan, everyone was loud; everyone talked with their hands. Everyone had a mother or sister or aunt or cousin who was a short and curvy Puerto Rican woman with wild curls and an intense face.

Papi, Carlos, and I sat on the row of chairs with all the luggage. Papi dozed, and Carlos and I pulled out our shopping bag from the newsstand. Papi had bought a comic book for Carlos and logic puzzles for me.

After twenty minutes, Mami was visibly calmer.

"Good talk with Jerrold?" Papi asked.

"You're not mad anymore?" Carlos asked.

Mami smiled and kissed him on the forehead. "I wasn't really mad," she said. "I was scared. I just needed to talk it through with him."

"You seemed mad," Carlos said.

"What did he say?" I asked.

"He shared all the information he'd gotten," Mami said. "I can't be specific, but I would have come to the same conclusion."

"Good work, querida," Papi said. Then to us kids: "What do I always say? 'Good teams have good communication.' And whenever there's a problem, you gotta talk it out."

"Right now the team is hungry," I said. "Can good teams also have good food? Like, can we get a last Puerto Rican meal before we go home?"

We ate on the plane. I took my first bite of the fried mashed plantains with tomato sauce and shrimp after we took off. Mofongo is hard to find in LA. I asked Mami to get some extra to go, but she says it doesn't reheat very well.

The captain had just turned off the seat belt sign, and Papi and Carlos had gone to the lavatory.

Mami was doing some work. On her phone, she had a photo of a guy in shades and a baseball cap. The shot was a little blurry, and he had dark stubble on his face. On her laptop were pages and pages of what looked like mug shots, guys facing front who fit the same description.

"You looking for that guy?" I asked, indicating the man on the phone.

She nodded wearily.

"You just passed him," I said. "Scroll back up."

"What?" She sat up sharply. "You saw him?"

"Yeah," I said. I wiped my hand on an airline napkin and ran my index finger down her screen.

"Him," I said, pointing to a shot of what was obviously the same man, but without the cap or shades, and with blond hair.

Mami looked back and forth between the photo on her phone and the one on her computer screen.

"I think you're right," she said, openmouthed. "How did you catch that?"

"I don't know," I said. "Something about the lines." I shrugged. "The line of his jaw. The way his nose sits in his face. The cheekbones."

"The stubble didn't throw you off?"

"Not really," I said. "I wasn't looking at the color. Just the shapes and the structure of the features."

"Incredible," she said.

When Papi came back, Mami gave Carlos a tablet with headphones to watch a video. Then she shared what I'd done.

Papi looked between the pictures. "Wow. I would have missed that, too."

Weird. Could they really not see what I saw?

"I didn't see this coming," Mami said. "We need to tell Jerrold."

"Tell him what?" I asked. "That I matched up two photos?"

"Seriously, corazón," Mami said. "This is an unusual ability. And you may be able to help the Factory by making connections that others don't see."

"Cool," I said. "Can I go back to my food?"

"Sure, amor," Mami said.

I settled back to enjoy the mofongo as the plane flew over the Gulf of Mexico.

During our layover in Dallas, we got word that El Rubio's briefcase contained evidence to incriminate some real estate guys whose cryptocurrency fortunes were linked to human trafficking.

Instead of commissioning an architect to design a luxury hotel, El Rubio's money will go to his defense for his upcoming criminal trial.

We got to our house in LA around 9 p.m. Pacific time, midnight in Puerto Rico. Everyone was jet-lagged. Carlos was wired and playing video games, something my parents rarely let him do. But they were both lying on the couch. Mami was scrolling through the news on her phone, and Papi was flipping channels on the TV.

I was lying on my bed, watching Deza's latest music video. Actually, I wasn't watching anymore, because I had fallen asleep, not *during* the video but during the behind-the-scenes interview with the director.

"Andréa," Mami called from the living room, waking me up. "Your phone is ringing."

"Let it ring," I said. Through bleary eyes, I saw the incoming-call notice pop up on my tablet, too.

"It's Jerrold," she said.

I always pick up for our handler with the Factory. Jerrold not only supervises us in the field; he also gives us our assignments and debriefs us. But this time, I felt too exhausted.

"Tell him I'm sleeping," I yelled. "For the rest of the year. I'll debrief next January."

"One good night of sleep ought to be enough," Mami said. "How about you debrief tomorrow?"

"Fine," I said. "Tell him I'll call him in the morning."

I rolled over and snuggled deeper under the covers.

I woke again twenty minutes later when Mami came into my room.

"Amor," she said touching my shoulder. "Wake up. Jerrold needs to talk to you."

"Can you bring me my phone?" I whined.

When Papi appeared in the doorway, it wasn't with my cell—it was with our landline. Something we almost never use. "It's Jerrold," Papi said, handing me the phone.

What could he be calling about so urgently?

I put the phone to my ear. "Hello, Jerrold," I said.

Papi and Mami closed the door behind.

"Sorry to bother you so soon after your last assignment," he said. "I couldn't reach you on your cell, and this couldn't wait. Did I wake you?"

"I was awake," I lied. "What's up?"

"I'm downstairs," he said. "Are you up for taking a ride?"

"Downstairs?" I asked. "You're here?"

"I'm here."

"Sure," I said. "I'll come down. My mom or dad ought to be free to join us."

"No need," he said. "I let them know this is a confidential conversation."

"Oh," I said, a knot forming in my chest. "Okay." Why just me? Had I done something wrong in Puerto Rico? Was there some kind of problem?

I grabbed a sweater and caught up with Mami in the living room. "Um, I'm having a one-on-one with Jerrold."

"I know," Mami said.

"Am I in trouble?" I asked.

Mami laughed. "No, cariño," she said. "You're fourteen. You're a full agent now."

THREE

LA was quiet as I walked down the steps of our house. The night was mild, so unlike the humid nights in Puerto Rico. Across the street, a man jogged by with a huge dog.

At the curb, a familiar dark sedan idled. I swallowed as I crossed the sidewalk and opened the back door of the car. I was relieved to see that Jerrold was smiling. We didn't hug or anything, but I immediately relaxed. I had known him for a year, and I knew that he didn't fake smile. He wore his usual dark three-piece suit.

My parents had been working for his organization for nearly twenty years, long before I was born. It's actually not just one organization. The International Alternative Intelligence Consortium (IAIC), or "the

Factory," is an association of several intelligence organizations of people of color. We aren't affiliated with any government, although we have a worldwide network with friends in the FBI and CIA and other government agencies.

The Factory uses different nonviolent strategies. Its members are trained in weapons, tradecraft, and self-defense. We gather information and leak it to the press. We help whistleblowers. There are several democratically elected Latin American leaders alive today because of us.

"Nice work in Puerto Rico," Jerrold said. "I'm sorry you had to make use of your skateboard. The Factory got you a new one, since you lost it in the line of duty."

"Thank you," I said, a bit confused. Surely he hadn't gotten me out of bed to deliver a skateboard.

The driver pulled the car away from the curb. At least, I assumed there was a driver. The partition was up and it was tinted dark, reflecting my tired-looking face back to me.

"I apologize for intruding on your downtime," Jerrold said. "We have a possible assignment for you."

"Me?" I asked. I felt nervous, but I knew I'd say yes to anything he asked.

"You'd be the lead agent," he said. "You'd be doing the bulk of the undercover work."

I nodded and tried to look serious. But inside I was like, *Wow! My! First! Assignment!*

"We need to get some information from a teenager in Arizona," he said. "If you say yes, you'll be on the next flight to Phoenix tomorrow."

"Does she live in Phoenix?" I asked. "The girl I need to get info from?"

"It's a boy," Jerrold said. "And he lives in Carson, Arizona."

"A boy?" I asked. "Am I supposed to . . . I don't know . . . try to . . . date him or something?"

I had never had a boyfriend. Never been kissed.

Jerrold shook his head. "Nothing like that," he said. "We just need access to his cell phone and laptop. Maybe some old family photos, if you can get them. We'll put you in classes with him, and you'll befriend him."

"Okay," I said. "What does the Factory know about him?"

"He's the son of a suspected terrorist," Jerrold said. "We have reason to believe that his father's planning an attack on a target somewhere in the southwestern US, but we can't find the father's location or the location of the attack. We've been passing on intel to our contacts at the FBI, but their supervisors aren't acting on it." From the tightening of his jaw, I could see he was angry about that.

"The young man's parents have been separated for over a decade. They never officially divorced. I emphasized to your mother that our sources haven't found any evidence that the father is in contact with the mother or son. We don't expect trouble. You'd mostly be getting intel from his devices. We're hoping a younger operative might be able to gain his trust and maybe get him to say something about his father that could give us a clue about his location."

"Why me?" I asked. "Don't you have teen operatives who are more experienced?"

"We do," Jerrold said. "But not many the right age." He looked out the window, toward the hills past Montebello. "Of our high school first- and second-years, we think you'd be the best fit."

I had the distinct feeling there was something he wasn't telling me.

"How come?" I asked. "Does he only speak Spanish? Am I the one Spanish-speaking operative my age at the Factory?" But how could that be? We're all people of color—there had to be others.

"Actually," Jerrold said. He stopped and pursed his lips. He always did this before he made the decision to give more info. "It's sort of the opposite. You would be the best fit because you can easily be mistaken for white."

"I'm not white," I said.

"I know that," Jerrold said. "But he wouldn't."

"He would know the moment I opened my—" I broke off. I was a spy. I could change my way of speaking, my name, my mannerisms.

I looked at our images in the tinted-glass partition. In the reflection, Jerrold had coffee-brown skin and black hair in tight circles the circumference of my pinkie. Through his rimless glasses, I could see his eyes were a dark brown, almost black. Mine were lighter brown.

My skin was tawny since our trip to Puerto Rico, but I'd been paler during the winters when we were living on the East Coast. My hair was sandy brown. I had springy curls, but if I pulled my hair back in a bun, it looked straight. Between the curly hair and hoop earrings and the fact that half the time I wore fútbol (excuse me, *soccer*) or other sports jerseys for Mexico or Puerto Rico, nobody ever thought I was anything but Latina. But I guess most of those were things I could change: hair, clothes, jewelry.

No matter what Jerrold wore or how he did his hair, he could never pass for anything but Black. But I could.

"It's not an easy request," he said. "That's why I wanted to talk to you directly. It's a heavy burden to have to give up who you are to go undercover."

"Why does this kid need to think I'm white?"

He hesitated, his eyes straying out the window to the traffic going in the other direction. "His father's a white supremacist," Jerrold said. "Whatever his father has planned, it's about targeting Black or brown or Jewish folks."

I took a deep breath.

Nine months before, Carlos had woken up early and come into the living room. Papi had fallen asleep over his briefing materials at the kitchen table. White supremacist website printouts. They wanted to kill Black and brown people. Lock people up for the color of their skin and shoot anyone brown at the borders.

Carlos panicked. Papi woke and found him crying. The crying woke me up, and I stumbled into the living room.

Papi took the printouts from Carlos's hands. But not before I looked over his shoulder and saw some of the words in all capital letters.

"Are these people really going to do all this?" Carlos asked him.

"No, querido," he said. "These are extremists."

"But they're on the internet talking about killing people," I said. "Isn't that against the law? Shouldn't somebody make them take down that website?"

Papi sighed. "A lot of people agree with you," he said. "Many of us are working to stop them. Including me and Mami. This is a big part of what we do at the Factory."

Papi put his arms around Carlos and motioned for me to join. Carlos stopped crying. We both felt reassured by Papi's words, and safe in his strong brown arms. Papi put the papers away and made us pancakes.

After that, Papi read his briefing materials only inside his study, and I didn't hear any more about it.

If this terrorist was posting those kinds of hateful messages, then he needed to be stopped. I was committed to doing what needed to be done. But I also remembered the hateful language on the website, and the knot in my chest came back.

I swallowed. "I'm in."

FOUR

The Factory didn't know where John Summer was. Only that he had posted the message from an internet café in Utah, and that he used to live in Arizona, where he still had a son.

Jerrold handed me a tablet. "This," he said, "is the only visual evidence we have of the terrorist." On the screen was video footage from a security camera.

"This was taken at a storage unit outside Boise, Idaho," Jerrold said.

The image was a grainy black-and-white. It showed a plain hallway with roll-up doors along both walls. After about thirty seconds, there was movement. A tall man walked past the camera in dark clothes. He glanced up toward the camera briefly.

Jerrold stopped the video so I could see as the camera captured the man's full face. His eyes were hidden behind large shades that also hid the tops of his cheekbones. The lower half of his face was obscured by a full beard. He had on an army cap over longish hair.

"That storage unit turned out to be filled with guns and explosives," Jerrold said. "And it was rented to John L. Summer, with an Oregon address. The address was fake, but the weapons were real. The FBI confiscated all of them."

"And this was the only footage of him?" I asked.

"The only footage that survived," Jerrold said. "He must have come to the storage space in person when he rented it in the first place, but the security company wipes their backups every six months, so there's no video of that visit. He probably knew their schedule and planned accordingly—this guy is a real pro."

"It's obvious that he sees the camera," I said.

Jerrold nodded. "But he seems confident that between the shades, the beard, and the hat, he's unrecognizable."

Jerrold swiped to the next photo on the tablet. "We also have this old driver's license picture of him that he's posted with some of his manifestos."

I looked into the face of a blond, white guy in his twenties. He was unsmiling but didn't have any of the malice in his face that you would expect from a potential mass murderer. Which goes to show, you never really know about people.

"But that's where the trail ends," Jerrold said. "He

doesn't have a current driver's license in Arizona or Utah, and we haven't been able to track down his residence."

Jerrold swiped back to the previous image. "This is all just background. You won't be dealing with him at all, just befriending his estranged son."

I stared at the blank lenses of the man's shades. I was glad I wouldn't be going up against him.

"Even though I'm the main operative, my family would travel with me, right?" I asked. "Like usual?"

Jerrold shook his head. "That would be the other big change."

"I'd travel alone?" I asked, panicked. I wanted to take this guy down, but by myself? At fourteen? Or was his son at some kind of boarding school?

"You would travel with your mother," Jerrold said.

"What about my dad and brother?" I asked.

"They'd stay in Los Angeles," he said. "At least initially. We might bring them onto the team if the assignment stretched on for a while."

"But how come—?" I broke off and looked at my reflection again. Papi was Mexican and looked Indigenous. Mami was Puerto Rican but much lighter skinned. I had an echo of Papi's slanting eyes, but my brother got Papi's brown skin and full-on Indio features.

The African American scholar W. E. B. Du Bois said, "The problem of the twentieth century is the problem of the color line." In the twenty-first century, it looked like the color line had been drawn across my family.

"Before I get final approval from your parents, I wanted you to have the whole picture," Jerrold said. "It's critical to stop him. He posted threats to unleash some kind of 'localized Armageddon' this summer on what he calls 'dark intruders.' He's taken down the web page, but not before some of our people got a screenshot. They took the evidence to some trusted allies in the FBI. Unfortunately, the Bureau had 'other priorities.' With the web page down, they refused to call it a credible threat. I know you've just gotten back from another operation. Do you need time to think it over?"

"Absolutely not," I said. "We've gotta stop this guy."

And that was how I, Andréa Hernández-Baldoquín, and my mother, Bárbara Baldoquín-Mendoza, found ourselves traveling to Carson, Arizona, as Andrea and Barbara Burke. Operatives often use their same first names. But I'm used to being called Andréa with a Spanish pronunciation: ahn-DRAY-ah, with a hard Spanish r that sounds like a soft d. (If people couldn't do the hard r, I would settle for the right phonetic vowels.) Introducing myself with the English pronunciation would take some getting used to.

At the LA airport, Papi squeezed me tight and kissed me on the forehead. Carlos is not usually one for displays of affection, but he hugged me, too.

"I'm gonna miss you," I said. "Who's gonna annoy me and steal my sausages at breakfast?"

He shrugged, but his eyes were extra shiny. We'd never been apart before. Mami or Papi would sometimes travel, but Carlos and I always stayed together. I leaned in and hugged him again as Mami fussed at Papi. I still wasn't used to seeing her with blond hair, or either of us with our hair straightened.

"Don't forget that Carlos's online Decolonial D&D group is on a two-week break," Mami said. "But no going crazy with video games."

Papi nodded solemnly.

"I put his dentist appointment in your calendar," Mami added.

"I've got it," Papi said. "You'll remind me, anyway. It's not like you're going off the grid in the jungle, querida. You can just text me."

Mami nodded. Papi hugged her, and they kissed on the lips. Not a super-mushy kiss, but not just a quick peck, either.

Mami hugged Carlos again.

"You all need to get going," Papi said. "You still need to pass through security."

Papi gave me one last squeeze.

Mami and I walked down an expedited lane to the TSA agent who would check our IDs. It was on the outer edge of the security area, so Papi and Carlos were able to walk alongside us.

The woman on the tall stool looked at our documents and waved us through.

We set all our stuff on the conveyor belt and stood in line for the security screening.

I looked over my shoulder to see Carlos still waving. I waved back.

Just before I stepped into the metal detector, I heard Papi call, "I love you, Andréa."

I turned and blew him a kiss, and then another TSA agent beckoned me to step through.

It was like a portal to a new identity. I would need to get used to being ANN-dree-yuh, teenage white girl.

FIVE

Calvin Coolidge High School is a row of squat brick buildings beside an athletic field and surrounded by a chain-link fence. The school takes up a whole block in what the city of Carson ambitiously calls downtown. There's a small collection of shops, including a post office, a grocery store, a diner, and a hairdresser . . . and apparently things got shaken up when the coffee shop/bookstore started selling comic books and allowing teens to play games. Two blocks away there's a strip mall, but that's about all the activity I could find.

Our cover story was that my parents were getting a divorce and we were moving from LA to Arizona, to my "great-aunt's" house. Supposedly, she was our favorite relative who happened to be out of town for three months on a world tour.

So my blond mom enrolled me—her sandy-haired daughter—in the local public high school under the name Andrea (ANN-drea) Burke. I was supposedly transferring from a private school in LA, the Penfield Academy. I'd read through their glossy brochures in my briefing materials. Since I had a (fake) prep school background, the principal at Calvin Coolidge didn't worry that I would be behind in all the ninth-grade classes.

I started ninth grade in the middle of June, the most random time to start a new school. It was unusual to start so late, but it's public school. Anyone can enroll if they have the right address. At least it was a year-round school, so I wasn't showing up just in time for the end of the term. It looked pretty ridiculous, but the whole assignment was a long shot. I was the operative of last resort. Their "Hail Mary" play.

I walked into the school office with Mami. I mean, my mom. It was hard to get used to thinking in English all the time. The blond student behind the desk perked right up.

"You must be the new girl," she said, looking over my trendy pale cotton top and light jeans. "I'm Mandy, the second-period office aide."

"We literally flew into town yesterday," Mom said in a voice that still sounded strange to me. We had practiced being Barb and ANN-drea during the whole plane ride. "I spoke on the phone with the principal."

"Oh, yes," the girl said. "We have your schedule all ready for you. You'll just have to come back at the end of the day when the secretary is here, to get a locker assignment."

She stood and picked up a pair of hall passes. "I can show you around."

I said goodbye to my mom—Barb!—and walked down the hallway of the two-story building. There wasn't that much to see. We passed a square cafeteria with bench tables and an industrial food smell.

"Here's what you really need to know," Mandy said. "Our type of girls sit in the corner near the window. We call it the First-Class Cabin. No flight attendants, but it's away from the kitchen smells and the unwashed masses. And we get special food. The stuff they serve is inedible piles of salt and sugar. Except Mexican Meal Monday. The tacos are the best, and we had a petition, so now they'll also do them as a bowl, without the carbs."

I wasn't quite sure what to say. I'd never worried about carbs before. Mandy was much slimmer than me, with a similar trendy top and pale blue jeans. She wore all her clothes much tighter than I did. Did they cut off her circulation? As it was, I felt a bit claustrophobic in my disguise. I was usually a jersey-and-loose-jeans kind of girl. Or maybe athletic shorts.

As she walked me down the hall to my class, a knot of Spanish-speaking teens came in through a side door.

I opened my mouth to greet them automatically, but then caught myself and closed it.

"Do you all have a hall pass?" Mandy asked. "If the principal catches you again, it'll be an automatic suspension."

The group rolled their eyes and ignored her, but she was unfazed. It took me a moment to realize that she didn't understand the word "pendeja," which one boy muttered loud enough for us to hear. As I glanced back, I saw a girl in a short skirt and dark eyeliner look me up and down with a scowl. I looked at Mandy and me, in light-wash jeans and pastel-colored tees. We looked like we belonged together. I swallowed the lump in my throat and let Mandy show me to my history class.

Kyle Summer sat in front of me. Did our organization have influence over high school seating charts, or did I just luck out? I observed him carefully and a bit nervously. Did he share his dad's beliefs? It was impossible to tell. He had the kind of platinum-blond hair most white kids grow out of, and a narrow frame. He didn't raise his hand during class, so I didn't get to hear his voice. He wore torn jeans but not torn, like, stylishly. They were torn like when you fall off your bike and tear the knees, but you just keep wearing the jeans and don't care. He had on a T-shirt with something printed on it that I couldn't see.

"The US Constitution was heavily influenced by

the English Constitution," the teacher said, and wrote "Magna Carta" on the board. He went on and on about how amazing the English system was.

My parents had taught me that a whole lot of the ideas in the US Constitution had come from the Iroquois Constitution, particularly concepts that the English had never thought about. Like that leaders were servants of the people, not their masters. And the idea of impeachment if a leader broke the rules. Even ideas like freedom of expression and illegal searches.

But the Calvin Coolidge High School history teacher didn't mention any of that. It was England, England, England. What did I expect from Arizona, the state that had voted to outlaw ethnic studies and critical race theory? I wanted to say something, but ANN-drea definitely wouldn't be rocking this boat. To amuse myself, I translated everything the teacher said into Spanish. Even if nobody here knew who I was, I knew.

When the bell rang, I leaned forward and tapped Kyle on the shoulder. It was time to put Operation Befriend Kyle into action. "Can you tell me how to get to Mr. Halbersham's class?" I was hoping he would offer to walk me there, but instead he just muttered, "To the right and down the stairs," and scuttled away. So much for making friends.

The whole ninth grade had lunch at the same time, so I was planning to try to sit with him then. I got in the long cafeteria line and spotted him right away: twenty kids ahead of me. Hopefully, there'd be an empty seat at his table.

Soon, Kyle got a pair of hard-shell tacos and squeezed into a pretty full table. I tried to calculate whether I could squeeze in. Would it be too obvious? Was there more room at other tables? Maybe a seat at a table nearby?

But then Mandy took my arm and pulled me out of the line. "No, no, no," she said. "We don't wait in the Mexican Meal Monday line. We have a special order. I got an extra bowl for you. Have your mom tell the principal you're gluten-free." She whisked me over to the First-Class Cabin. What did she mean she got me an extra bowl? Did that mean that a kid with a legit gluten issue didn't get their lunch? My mom said a lot of people of color had problems with the standard US diet. I wanted to object, but I didn't want to blow my cover as a white girl. Also, I needed somewhere to sit. I didn't know anyone else, and Kyle's table was full anyway.

Mandy introduced me to four other girls with willowy shapes and similar fashion choices. Each of us had a tray with a large portion of chopped romaine lettuce, covered in a scoop of taco meat and a scoop of beans. On the side was a hard taco shell, some salsa, and a plastic container of rice. I watched as each girl dumped the rice into the trash. Did they expect me to dump my rice? I was definitely going to eat the rice.

"How's your first day?" Mandy asked.

"See any cute boys?" the girl next to her asked.

"Not yet," I said. Was Kyle cute? Not my type. Too pale. But he had attractive features. Big eyes, and the contrast with his porcelain skin made the natural color in his lips more noticeable.

"I sat toward the front, so I didn't get to study many of them," I said.

Mandy ate her food in tiny bites.

"He was in my class," I said, pointing out Kyle as he stood up to get a napkin. I recognized the image on his shirt. "The one in the Arantxa superhero tee."

"That whole group of boys is definitely on the no-fly list," Mandy said. "We'll find you someone cute."

"But if he's an athlete, ask first," another girl said. "Most of them have been spoken for."

"Girls' code," Mandy said. "But just talk to me. I know everyone here, and which football and basketball players belong to the girls on our squad."

"Mandy's mom is Lydia Charles from Channel Four News," one of the girls said. "We get the best gossip before anyone else."

Mandy smiled. "I'm sort of like the mayor of the school," she said.

I nodded.

"How'd you end up in Carson?" one of the other girls asked.

"I'm from LA," I said. "My parents are getting

divorced, and me and my mom moved here to live in my great-aunt's house."

"Where'd you go to school before?" another girl asked.

"Penfield Academy," I said.

"I've heard of it," Mandy said. "You definitely belong in First Class."

"I hated the uniforms," I said. "And the homework. But otherwise, it was okay."

"I'm sure the food was better," the first girl said.

"I don't know yet," I said. With all the questions, my plate was still untouched. Obviously, I couldn't just dig into the rice in front of them. Maybe I could smuggle it out.

"Let the girl eat," Mandy said.

I put some salsa on my salad and broke off a tiny piece of the hard-shell taco to scoop up some of the beans. But when I ate it, I almost choked. Everyone had been excited about Mexican Meal Monday, even the teachers. They had used the word "taco." My mind said "taco." But what my mouth tasted was an industrial version of the dish my Mexican family made so deliciously.

The worst part wasn't the chalky refried beans or the taco shell like cardboard. It wasn't even the packets of "authentic" salsa that tasted more like ketchup. The worst part was the fact that I couldn't say anything about it. I couldn't stand up in the middle of Calvin

Coolidge High School and throw my plastic tray on the floor, yelling, "You call these tacos? My tía Rosa makes real tacos. From scratch. With masa. From a recipe handed down from our great-grandmother in Oaxaca." But I was supposed to be white.

Dang! I needed to fit in. But even as a spy, you can't deny something obvious. *No, I'm not standing in your hallway with the door to your wall safe open. No, I'm not underneath your car with a blowtorch. No, this isn't a gun in my hand. No, I'm not ready to throw up your precious Mexican Meal Monday bowl.*

I couldn't backpedal and fix my face and say, "Yum, so great and only two hundred calories!" So I moved the food around the plate listlessly.

"We had more authentic Mexican food in LA," I said. "I miss my old life."

"But the downside to authentic Mexican food is that you need authentic Mexicans to make it," one of the girls said.

Everyone laughed.

I was about two seconds behind. A sort of chuckle through my nose, with my mouth full of fake food.

I needed to make friends with Kyle fast, not only to stop the terrorist but also so that I could get out of First Class and back to the economy seating with my people.

SIX

All day, I failed utterly to connect with Kyle. I'd only learned more than I ever wanted to know about the low-carb lifestyle as Mandy followed me around. But luckily, that night was PTA night. The school was open, and that would give us a chance to search Kyle's locker. Maybe it would give me some insight into his personality to help me to make friends with him. Or better yet, maybe he had some secret family photo in there that included his dad.

Mom and I pulled up to Calvin Coolidge a little after seven. Two women walked into the school, wearing pastel blouses. Maybe they were the mothers of a couple of First-Class girls.

It was still light out, but Mom and I waited for them

to enter before we got out of the car. Both of us were wearing hooded sweatshirts, and we didn't want those two mothers to call the cops on us, or to ask who we were and why were we coming to PTA night.

Once we were in, instead of heading down the hall to the meeting in the school library, we went around the corner to the main office.

I pulled the lock picks out of my pocket. I was less experienced than Mom, but she wanted me to get practice in real-life situations, and the stakes here were lower than they would be if there were an actual terrorist in the vicinity.

The trick to picking a lock is patience and chill. You can't let the lock psych you out. If you get nervous, your hands shake, and the tool can't get the right purchase inside the lock. Or your palms sweat and the pick slips. You often don't get it on the first few tries; it takes a while to get to know each lock. You can't panic. "Breathe and believe"—that's what Mom had taught me.

I forced myself not to jump at every sound. Cars going by out on the street. A burst of laughter from the PTA meeting around the corner and down the hall. *Breathe and believe.*

It was probably three minutes, but it felt like much longer. Finally, the lock clicked, and the door opened.

The lights were out in the main office, and we had to use flashlights. I made sure not to bump into any of the furniture as I made my way to the secretary's computer.

The desktop computer took a moment to boot up. When I got to the log-in screen, I typed the code that I had secretly recorded on my phone when the school secretary had logged in to give me my locker assignment: 3651. Four dots showed up on the screen. I expected the welcome to pop up like it had for her, but it didn't. I tried again, not rushing this time: 3-6-5-1. It failed again.

"Mom, it's not working," I said.

Mom was picking the lock on the cabinet that held student files.

"How can that be?" she asked. "I transcribed it myself."

Mom opened her phone and pulled up the video I had sent her. The screen glowed eerily in the dark office.

Mom played the slo-mo video, and I watched the secretary's lacquered pink nails tap the keyboard. Three . . . six . . . five . . . one. I blinked. That was the sequence I had tried. Twice. It hadn't worked.

"Could they have changed the code?" I asked.

"That seems unlikely," Mom said. "It's high school, not the CIA."

"Can you slow it down even more?" I asked.

"I think so," Mom said. "I'll play the slo-mo on slo-mo."

She tapped several keys, and the video slowed to a crawl. And then we saw it: a gentle double-tap on the five key.

I turned back to the computer. I keyed in 3-6-5-5-1 and held my breath.

The welcome screen came up.

"Nice work," Mom said.

I smiled and scrolled down to *S* for Summer.

It took a while to find the locker assignments and look up Kyle's, 487. I wasn't sure where that was, but we'd find out. The combination was there, too, and I memorized it.

I shut down the computer, and we crept out of the office. The hallway was empty. We heard voices from the stairwell. We pulled back and listened. The voices were heading away from us and up the stairs.

We walked down the main hallway, where locker numbers were in the hundreds. Down a corridor to the left, they were in the six hundreds. We backtracked and turned to the right and found the four hundreds.

I used the combination from the main office computer to get into Kyle's locker. I swallowed hard and pulled up on the locking mechanism. I was worried the combo wouldn't work and wondered what I would or wouldn't find.

The door swung open, and it was . . . completely lacking in personality. A pile of books and notebooks and three energy bars. I snapped pictures so I could put it all back the same way. I took the books and note-books out, looking underneath for anything interesting. Nothing personal. On the one hand, I was relieved not to see white supremacist manifestos or anything, but, on the other hand, there was nothing I could use to get to know him.

I took the books and notebook and put them into a nylon bag I'd had in my sweatshirt pocket. Then Mom kept lookout by Kyle's locker while I went to inspect Kyle's stuff. I slipped into the girl's bathroom for privacy, locked myself into the last stall, and sifted through the pages.

They were just schoolbooks. There was nothing scrawled in the margins. The notebook had only notes for class. *The Scarlet Letter*. Algebra. The Thirteen Colonies. Not even a doodle. Certainly nothing related to white supremacy, his dad, or terrorism.

I was about to head out of the bathroom when two women entered. I pulled my feet up, so I was squatting, fully clothed, on the toilet seat.

"Do you know what he said to me outside the meeting, though?" one woman asked the other.

I'd wait until they left and then sneak out.

"He said it in confidence," the woman said, "but . . ."

"Come on, tell me."

"Okay, wait."

I heard a pair of heels clacking my way. I caught glimpses of feet and heard her opening one stall door after another.

I pulled out my phone and readied myself to spring off the toilet seat. As she opened the door next to me, I flipped the latch and leaped out of the stall.

"I don't care if you ground me for the rest of my life, Mom!" I yelled into the phone. "Eventually, I'll turn eighteen and I'll go live with Dad." From that first day in the Texas hotel when Mom had me think on my feet, I've learned to use my alternate personality, "Michelle," as a cover.

I kept my hoodie pulled down over my face and barreled out of the bathroom.

As the door closed behind me, I heard one woman say, "Hormones." Adults always believe the biggest stereotypes about teen girls.

I dashed back through the hallway with the bag under one arm, looking over my shoulder, just in case, but no one was following me, and I managed to put Kyle's belongings back in his locker without being seen.

As Mom and I headed out through the school's front doors, we heard voices behind us. The PTA meeting was letting out.

We didn't wait for women in pastel to ask us any questions. We hustled into the car and peeled out of the parking lot. Mom drove quickly, but not so fast as to attract attention.

I told her about the big amount of nothing I had found.

"We struck out," she said. "It happens."

"I guess," I said. "Although . . . why wouldn't you have anything in your locker . . . unless you had something to hide?"

SEVEN

When **we got back** to the great-aunt's house, I collapsed onto the beige couch, and Mom sat on the matching armchair. I missed our house in California with its bright Mexican and Puerto Rican art and the dark leather couch that didn't show dirt. I tried to kick back, but there were pillows with cartoon puppies on them, and across from the door was a curio cabinet with porcelain figures of big-eyed animals. It felt like everything was watching me.

The house was nestled on a tree-lined street two miles from the high school. It had been recently painted white with light blue trim. The lawn was neatly mowed. It was nice enough, but it felt more like a quirky guesthouse than someone's home. The actual woman who lived there was "retired" and "a world traveler." In other words, a spy. I overheard Jerrold tell my mom she was on a mission in Afghanistan.

I went upstairs to the bedroom to relax. There were no watching animals in the room we shared, thankfully. My twin bed was against one wall, and Mom's was against the other, under the window. I thought I'd just lie down for a few minutes, but when I woke up, it was three in the morning.

Moonlight streamed in through the crack between the curtains. I couldn't really see my mother, but I detected the outline of her shape on the bed. I heard the faint and regular breathing of deep sleep.

"Mom?" I whispered into the dark.

"Yes, dear?" she said. Wow, Mom was a good spy. Usually she would respond in Spanish. I was impressed that she could remember her cover, even when woken up out of a sound sleep.

"He looks so ordinary," I said. "Kyle does. It's so creepy to think his dad's a white supremacist."

"Just because his dad is, it doesn't mean he is, dear," Mom said. It made the whole situation creepier, Mom calling me these white pet names. She never called me "dear" at home.

"I'm not sure how to get him to talk to me," I said. "And in the meantime, I have to keep laughing along with these snobby girls when they spout insults about Mexicans."

Mom nodded. I could see the movement of her head in the dark. "I've had assignments where they wanted me to pass for white. It's not easy. You hear all the stuff people say about us when they think we're not listening."

"Yeah," I said. "Do you think we can stop this guy?"

"I think if anyone has a shot at doing it, it's us."

"Why didn't the Factory just send someone white?" I asked. "Aren't there any white operatives in the network?"

Mom sighed. "Ten years ago, they had a deep-cover operation with a white supremacist. And it . . . it went badly. I helped them debrief the white operative."

"What happened?"

"Well . . ." Mom paused in that way I had come to recognize when she was trying to figure out what she could tell me about a classified operation. "Basically, the white nationalist guy was really cunning, and he figured out how to manipulate the operative."

"Like, into agreeing with him?" I asked.

"No, not at all," Mom said. "But into thinking that he wasn't so dangerous. At the key moment, the operative got confused because . . . well . . . she couldn't quite accept the kind of brutality that racist people are capable of. She had gotten to know the guy personally, which was part of the operation. And she was able to see the good in him. Which is fine. But she couldn't hold on to the idea of his goodness and the danger he represented at the same time. She thought she could redeem him."

"But she couldn't?"

"No," Mom said. "He blew himself up and took a whole Muslim school with him. Fortunately, we had evacuated it."

"Wow."

"With our operatives of color, even if we can pass for white, we're less likely to get confused about the dangers of racism. Even if it's muted in the ways we've felt it. When we've been connected to people and communities who have been devastated by racism, we're far less likely to underestimate the danger of white supremacists."

"Did you hesitate when Jerrold wanted to put me in the field on this one?" I asked.

I wished I could see her face, but I just heard the inhalation and exhalation of breath as she thought. "I worried for your safety. I always do. Even more after that chase in Puerto Rico. But you're not befriending a white supremacist. You're befriending his estranged son, who hasn't seen him in over a decade. Jerrold assured me that's the extent of the operation. So I separated my feelings as a mom from my feelings as an agent. As a mom, I know that we live in a brutal world where many people suffer or die, and it's my job to protect you. As an agent, it's my job to protect *everyone*, and I understand that agents take risks to do that. I asked Jerrold if there was anyone else we could send, or any other way to get a line on this guy. He told me that he had tried everything else. Kyle Summer seems like a quiet kid with no record of getting into trouble. His dad is a different story, but we're not likely to encounter him at all. I thought about the thousands or tens of thousands that might die or be injured if this guy succeeds. So I gave my approval."

Then I did something I felt I should be above as a spy. But Mom always said good spies ask for the support they need.

"Mom, can I sleep the rest of the night in your bed?"

"Of course," she said. She lifted up the covers for me to climb in.

Spy or no spy, I curled up next to my mother and went to sleep.

EIGHT

The next day, Kyle didn't speak a word in any of the three classes we had together. I did notice, however, that—unlike in his photo—he had braces. That didn't seem worthy of reporting. I shuffled from class to class, just like I had seen kids do on television. The whole school looked like something on TV, from the linoleum floors to the gray lockers to the cliques of students in the hallways.

I was bored and frustrated that I wasn't able to make any progress. The only welcome distraction came when my web programming class went to the library with some other classes for a presentation on internet safety, and I saw a really cute guy. I figured he was in a different year, because I would have noticed him if he had been at ninth-grade lunch. I would not be reporting his cuteness to the Factory. Or to the First-Class Cabin. He was Latino, his skin a rich brown, and he had long eyelashes and a twisted front tooth in his smile. Not the kind of boy who would fit with my pastel-wearing white-girl cover.

It was Pizza Tuesday, but instead of pizza, the girls each had just a short stack of pepperoni they put on their salads. "The key to the low-carb lifestyle is protein," Mandy explained. I looked longingly at the pizza. It wasn't like the rice—I couldn't smuggle it out and eat it later as a snack in the bathroom. I hadn't brought in a note from my mom that I was gluten-free, but Mandy had gotten me the salad meal, anyway.

My last class of the day was near the front door of the school, so I was planning to follow Kyle home, hoping that I would see *something* that might give me a clue about how to get past his reserve. But Mandy waylaid me in the hallway.

"We're going to the mall today," she said. "Wanna join us?"

We stepped out into the bright Arizona sunlight.

"I don't know," I said, stalling as we walked down the steps. "I have to ask my mom." I sent a fake text. Meanwhile, Kyle appeared, and I spotted him turning north on Main Street.

"Which way is the mall?" I asked.

"That way," Mandy said, pointing north. I didn't want to go to the mall with them. But depending on where Kyle was going, I'd be less conspicuous following him in a group. Maybe he was going to the mall, too. So I pretended my mom had said yes to my text.

The five of us walked down the street. Mandy was in full mayor mode, pointing out the boutique where her sister had bought a designer wedding dress and the hairdresser that did all their hair. I nodded, but the only one doing my hair would be my mom. Nobody else in Carson, Arizona, had clearance to know my natural hair texture.

As we walked down the street, I caught our reflection in the glass of a storefront. A knot of girls with hair that spanned from platinum blond to light auburn. Was that me in the center with the flat sandy hair? I didn't recognize myself. The eyes a little slanted, the lips a little full, but in context, I looked like a white girl.

"ANN-drea," Mandy said. It still took me a moment to remember that was my name. "You need to pay attention, or you'll end up as a hair-removal casualty. Like, their waxing is not the best. But their eyebrow threading is amazing. Since, no offense, obviously you haven't found a place here yet."

My eyebrows? Was I supposed to do something different with my eyebrows?

I tried to keep my hand from flying up and touching them. *Focus, ANN-drea,* I told myself. I saw Kyle turn down a side street.

"Which way is the mall from here, again?" I asked.

"Two more blocks down," Mandy said, and pointed straight ahead.

We reached the corner. Kyle was walking into a café, presumably the one with the comic books and board games.

"I gotta pee really bad," I said. "I'm going to quickly run into that café."

"We'll go ahead," Mandy said. "Meet you there."

"Let's try the café," one of the other girls said. "The coffee at the mall is not the best."

"Coffee shops mean calorie temptations," Mandy warned.

"Good point," I said. I didn't want them following me.

"We'll make a pact not to get anything bad," the other girl said.

I was not pleased to be seen with them, but at that point I had committed myself. I walked in with the crew.

The café had a dozen small tables. Against the far wall was the counter, with a menu written on a whiteboard overhead. On the adjacent wall were tall wooden shelves with books and games.

As I headed to the bathroom, Mandy squealed, "They have fat-free lattes with Splenda!"

I leaned forward so my hair was hanging in my face as I passed Kyle's table. He was sitting with his back to me. On the table was a coffee drink and a card game. He played cards! Maybe that was my way in. I tried to see what the game was, but I didn't have a good angle. I walked into the bathroom.

How long does it take to pee? I timed a minute, then washed my hands. On the way back, I lingered by the game shelf next to Kyle's table. I browsed, with my back toward him, then pulled out my phone and put the camera in selfie mode. I took several photos over my shoulder, then headed back to the counter.

"I was totally wrong," Mandy said. "This place isn't the diet danger zone—it's the promised land."

"Totally," another girl said. "Fat-free, no carb, sugar-free, and a caffeine kick for energy. What more could a girl want?"

I thought of several things but kept my head down as I followed them to the mall.

This is temporary, I reminded myself. The sooner I could befriend Kyle, the better.

NINE

It was weird, suddenly living with only half my family. I didn't take my personal phone to school, only my Factory cell for emergencies. But after I got back from the mall, I texted Papi and Carlos on my real phone. Carlos sent back a GIF of a big-eyed puppy waving that said, "I miss you."

I laughed out loud, and it only made me miss him more.

The GIF went perfectly with the cartoon animals in the great-aunt's house. Other than the images and figurines, the house was comfortable, with a big bedroom, a living room, and a dining room. I especially liked the breakfast nook, and that's where Mom and I sat to debrief. She had printed four of the photos I had taken of Kyle at the café, and we spread them out on the breakfast table.

The first thing I noticed was that Kyle had been drinking peppermint tea with milk, not coffee—I could see the little tag hanging out of his cup. But the main revelation was the image on the back of each playing card in front of Kyle: a large gold triangle.

"I've never seen that before," Mom said. "How about you?"

"I don't know," I said. "It seems familiar, but I can't place it."

We went online. "Golden triangle" was a geometry thing. There was also something in Southeast Asia.

I pulled out my phone and zoomed in on the image. There was lettering on one of the cards. The font made it look like some sort of ancient alphabet, but it also looked like it said "gulo." What the heck did that mean?

I looked up "gulo." It meant "mess" in one of the Filipino languages. It was also the scientific name for wolverines. I tried following that thread, but it led nowhere. Certainly not to a golden triangle. Maybe it was only part of the word?

"We managed to hack into John Summer's emails," Mom said. "But there's not much here. Mostly spam. He hardly uses this account. Just signs in a couple times a year to keep it active. Any luck?"

"Not yet," I said.

"It's funny," she said. "For some reason, he's getting a lot of spam in Spanish."

"I miss Spanish," I said. "It's so weird to be speaking English at home."

"I know," she said. "But we need to keep it up."

"Focus on the golden triangle, not the triángulo de oro," I joked.

Our eyes met. *Triángulo? Gulo?*

I went back online and there it was: Triángulo.

"I found it!" I yelled, and Mom looked on with me. Triángulo was a fantasy card game based on a series of comic books.

"¡Muy bien hecho, mi amor!" she said, then shook her head. "I mean, well done, dear." We laughed; she called Jerrold, and I went on to Wikipedia.

Triángulo Trading Cards. *See also* Triángulo comic series.

Triángulo is a trading card game and a comic book/ graphic novel series that began in 1998 from Comicultura. Originally one of countless derivatives of <u>Magic: The Gathering</u>, it became immensely popular in Latin America. US popularity has risen along with the crossover success of the superhero Arantxa and the Triángulo universe in Europe, particularly Spain. There are approximately thirty million Triángulo players worldwide, including an estimated fifteen million in the US.

Each game represents less of a battle, as in Magic, and more of a race. The players form two teams. Each team is acting out parts of the Triángulo Story.

I clicked the link to get the story synopsis.

Triángulo's origin story begins on a fictional Caribbean island called Caguama in the early 1600s, featuring three characters who create a spell that allows enslaved Africans to escape to a Maroon colony.

Cool. I clicked back to the explanation of the Triángulo game.

Each team is attempting to free the captives from slavery in the seventeenth century and to defeat a supervillain in the present era. Players take turns. Each team plays cards to reach their own goals and attempts to block, delay, or obstruct their opponent from reaching the same goal in their parallel world.

Since the game has come to the US, a new strategy called "Devil's Advocate" has come into fashion. The team tries to play exclusively on the side of the enslavers and villains, attempting to devastate the forces of good in the other team's game.

Yikes. Devil's Advocate sounded creepy. It was one

thing to play a game based on rescuing enslaved people, but to play on the other side was messed up. I wondered if that was the appeal to Kyle—whether he got kicks out of trying to capture people.

An organized tournament system is played at a national level in the US and several countries in Latin America. There is also a large reseller market for Triángulo cards. Certain cards can be valuable, due to their rarity and effectiveness in game play, and range in price from a few pennies to over a thousand dollars.

In a picture of a table shot from overhead, several cards lay faceup. A hand held a fan of cards. Each card had an intricate, brightly colored drawing. From the angle of the photo, I couldn't really see the image on the cards in the person's hand. The three cards facing up were Arantxa, the Basque Witch; Olumide, the Yoruba Priest; and BaguaNi, the Taino Bohique.

Arantxa was the only character in the game I had heard of. There was a movie and a popular book series about her. She had olive skin and wild curly hair. In the game, her character was drawn with a tattered soldier's uniform, where the wide-legged pants had been converted into a skirt. Olumide, the Yoruba Priest, had chocolate-brown skin, and her hair and body were wrapped in matching indigo cloth. She had a necklace of blue and clear beads. BaguaNi, the Taino Bohique, had jet-black straight hair. He wore a long loincloth of tan animal skin and had an *X* of cloth and feathers that hung across his otherwise bare chest.

I clicked to read more about the characters. In the origin story, the three of them weave together a spell that allows the captives to briefly fly and breathe underwater so they can escape from enslavement. Their magic all hinges upon their access to the triangle stone.

There were links to articles in the *New York Times* and various national magazines about how big Triángulo had gotten. And lots of pushback in the gaming community about what they called the "unwelcome Latin invasion." This controversy had been brewing for the last few years, and I had no idea. Wow, you can really miss a lot when you're homeschooled.

But if Kyle was a Triángulo fan, then that seemed like the best way to get to know him, which meant that I was going to become a Triángulo fan. Two hours later, a courier came to the house with an envelope full of comic books. I lay back on the couch to read.

"Really?" Mom said. "I'm up here trying to find secret white supremacist messages in spam for Viagra and you're reading comic books?"

"A spy's life is hard, Mom," I said, and sorted through the stack of comics to find the first one in the series.

TEN

The next day, we had free reading time in English class. Ms. Bellman's room had pictures of authors all over the walls. Shakespeare. Emily Dickinson. Agatha Christie. All of them white except for Amy Tan. On the back wall were a few posters that said "Everybody Reads!" One was for African American History Month. Another was for National Hispanic Heritage Month.

I pulled out my Triángulo book.

"Sorry, Ms. Burke," Ms. Bellman said. "No comics."

"It's not a comic," I said. "It's a Triángulo graphic novel." I made a point of saying the name so that Kyle couldn't miss it.

"No pictures," she said. "Print only."

"Sorry," I said, and pulled out my Shakespeare homework.

After class, Kyle came over to me.

"Where did you get that Triángulo book?" he asked. "It just came out, and the bookstore here doesn't have it. It's backordered online."

"I got it in LA," I lied. Or maybe it wasn't a lie. Jerrold's team must have found a copy somewhere— why not LA?

"Oh," he said. "You're new here, right?"

"Yeah," I said. "I just started."

"Well, um, could I maybe borrow it?" he asked. "Just over lunch."

"Sure," I said, and handed it to him.

"Don't worry," Kyle said. "I can give it back to you at the end of lunch."

We walked together toward the cafeteria.

"I'm surprised that you like this stuff," he said. "I thought you were the new First-Class girl."

"Are you kidding me?" I said. "When you're new, you sit with the first people who invite you. I'm sick of sitting at the calorie club. What's for lunch today?"

"Don't get too excited," Kyle said. "It's spaghetti."

"Can I take that as an invitation to sit with you?" I asked.

He shrugged. "Okay."

"I'm ANN-drea," I said.

"Kyle."

Success!

• • •

The spaghetti was as bad as he said, but at least it was filling. Kyle was terrible company, because he read the whole time, and the other people at his table stuck to themselves, too. I wasn't sure where to focus as I got alarmed looks from the First-Class girls.

When the bell rang, Kyle finally made eye contact. "Can I hang on to it until after school?" he asked.

"Sure," I said. "Keep it overnight if you want to finish it."

"Really?" Kyle asked. "Thanks. You know, people play Triángulo in the afternoon at the café."

"Cool," I said. Was he inviting me? Informing me? "Which café?" I asked.

"On Second Street," Kyle said. "The one you were in yesterday."

So much for being invisible. "I didn't even see you." The moment it came out of my mouth, it sounded wrong. Snobby. I wanted to clean it up somehow, but what could I say? *Actually, I saw you, too, because I was spying on you and took photos of your game?* This was all too awkward. Luckily, Kyle didn't look offended.

"See you," Kyle said, and we parted ways in the hall.

Later, between classes, Mandy ambushed me. "Look," she said. "Everyone slips on their diet sometimes. You don't have to be ashamed. Come back and sit with us. We'll support you. You don't have to slum with the losers by the kitchen."

"Mandy," I said, "I really appreciate you showing me around, but I've got other interests beside the low-carb lifestyle. Can I sort of . . . float between groups?"

Mandy, self-appointed mayor of the school, head of the First-Class girls in the cafeteria, looked at me sadly. "Do you know how many ninth-graders would kill to sit with us?"

"I just want to be free to talk to different people," I said.

"Suit yourself," she said icily, and strode down the hall.

ELEVEN

When I got to the café, Kyle was sitting at a table with another peppermint tea and milk.

"Can I join you?" I asked.

"Sure," he said.

I had barely sat down with him when the First-Class crew came in. Their giggles stopped when they saw me.

"Seriously?" one of them said.

They snagged the only open table by the door.

I got up to get a cup of tea for myself. Beside the counter was a bulletin board with a bunch of flyers and posters. The biggest and brightest one was for San Diego ComxCon. It had a typical comic-strip woman with a tiny waist, long legs, and big breasts. She basically looked like a brunette Barbie doll with a cape on.

As I waited for the barista to make my tea, Mandy came over.

"What are you doing?" she asked.

I looked from her to the Barbie superhero. *Looking at a poster of your body goals?* I wanted to say. But I didn't.

"Ordering tea," I said.

"No," she said. "What are you doing with that loser?"

"Bonding over comics," I said. "The game also seems pretty cool."

She opened her mouth to speak, but the barista was steaming milk, and the espresso machine was loud.

"Look," she said when the noise died down. "You might have been, like, a seven in Los Angeles, maybe an eight. But you could be a ten here in Carson. You could have any guy you want. You could be part of the homecoming court by the time you graduate. But not if you hang out with guys like that."

"Mandy," I began. I didn't know what to say. I knew what *I* wanted to say, but what would ANN-drea Burke say? The only person who mattered was Kyle. He was the assignment. He was the one whose confidence I needed to gain.

"I know I'm new in town," I said. A little loud so Kyle might hear. "You know how everything here works. But I like comics, and I'm making friends with people who like them, too. I hope you can respect that."

I headed back to Kyle.

Mandy marched after me. "No offense," she said.

"But I can't really respect your choice. It looks like a waste of time to me."

"If First Class is so great," I said, "why do you need to recruit? You all seem bored. Bored and hungry. Maybe if you read a comic book, you could imagine women aspiring to something more than being a size zero, getting a boyfriend, and being homecoming queen. No offense."

"Good burn," Kyle muttered.

"Let's get out of this café," one of the other girls said. "It's pretty gross in here."

"Yeah," Mandy agreed. "Smells like garbage."

The four of them flitted out like pastel butterflies.

"Sorry about that," I said. "I got some pink bubble-gum stuck to my shoe the first day, and I've had a little trouble getting it off."

Kyle laughed. "I think it's the first time in history anyone at Calvin Coolidge turned down the window clique for the nerds by the kitchen."

"Mandy couldn't quite accept my desertion," I said. "But I want to learn Triángulo. How do you play?"

Kyle grinned. My strategy had worked; I could see him relaxing with me. "Mandy thought you were slumming to be with me, but really, I'm the one slumming, teaching a novice."

"Ouch," I said. "Who's coming with the good burn now?"

"Aaaaanyway," Kyle said. "You have to buy cards.

You're trying to build up a good deck so that you can beat the other person. There are lots of the pretty generic cards. Like the Foliage cards. They can help block spells that get cast against you. But you have to have a lot of Foliage and be in a position to play it all at once. Then there are cards that are more helpful. Like the Taino Maroons. Or the African Maroons."

My parents had taught me about Maroons: African and Indigenous people who had run away from the colonizers and lived in the mountains or on the sea.

"Most of the Maroon cards are the same, except the high priest in the African Maroons, and the supreme priest in the Taino Maroons. And of course, the Basque Witch."

"Arantxa," I said. "Like in the comic book."

"Yes," Kyle said. "But there aren't any other Basque Maroons."

I wanted to say, *Yeah, because they didn't colonize Basque folks in the New World, only in Spain.* But ANN-drea Burke wouldn't know about that.

"The Arantxa card is so rare," Kyle said. "They come up for auction online and go fast . . . I heard one went for a thousand dollars."

He mixed the cards on the table.

"More specifically," Kyle went on explaining, "the seventeenth-century Arantxa card is really rare. The modern-day one is more common."

I kept scanning the way he talked about the cards

to see if there was a white supremacist undercurrent. But maybe he didn't just blurt out racist things when he first met someone.

"This game is being played simultaneously in the early 1600s and in present time. Another really powerful card is the one that switches you to the past or to the present," Kyle said. "Like, your opponent might have a really strong arsenal in one era but be weak in another. So if you can play a Time Travel card, you can totally get the better of them. Those cards are expensive, too."

I tried to draw out his thoughts about slavery. "How does it work?" I asked. "One side is the enslaver and the other is the three superheroes?"

Kyle shook his head. "In the usual setup, no one is the enslaver. The two teams play in parallel universes. Each team has their own enslaver and Maroon colony. As well as their present-time heroes and villain."

Kyle gestured to the cards. "You place obstacles in your opponent's path on behalf of their enslaver and modern villain, while they do the same to you."

"Okay," I said. "So you don't want the enslaver in the parallel universe to win? You just want him to delay the other team so that your team can win?"

"Yep," Kyle said. "That's the usual setup."

The usual setup. I kept waiting for him to say something about playing Devil's Advocate, but he didn't. I couldn't bring it up, because I was supposed to be new to all this. But if he didn't bring it up this time, I would pretend I'd gone home and googled it.

He brought out a small pack of cards that had characters on both sides. Kyle explained that these were basic character and place cards. They included a plain Triangle Stone card and an Ocean card with swirling waves on the side. There were also twenty cards of African and Taino characters, each pictured with machetes in a sugarcane field.

"So you need to buy a second deck?" I asked.

"The only thing you really need is the first deck," he said. "You could use anything for the characters and places. I heard that in poor countries, people play with, like, rocks and bottle caps to represent the different characters and places."

I tried to analyze the way he said "poor countries." Was it with contempt? Like the way certain racists talked about immigrants? Not exactly. But it wasn't respectful, either. Like how my mom always says people with lower incomes have to be smarter because they need to learn to be resourceful in order to survive.

"I like a second deck," Kyle said. "And the reason I come here instead of playing at home is that they have a real board."

He stood up from the table, went over to the game shelf, and pulled down a box. Inside was a thick piece of cardboard that folded into quarters. It had all the locations of the game: the Maroon colony, the sugar plantation, the modern-day world. And in the middle, where it said TRIÁNGULO, the Triangle Stone card fit perfectly in the center of the letter Á.

The whole board was laminated, so coffee drinks could go right on top of it.

"It's amazing," I said, running my fingers across the intricate designs.

"For my birthday, I'm gonna ask for a custom-made board," he said. "There are artists that will emphasize your favorite parts of the game."

He went back to explaining how the game worked. "When you play," Kyle said, "your goal is to free everyone from slavery. When you get them initiated with the necklace, they can get to the triangle stone and breathe underwater to get free." There was a little underwater area on the board.

He flipped through his deck and pulled out an Initiation card. It had a blue-and-white beaded necklace on it. He put it on one of the cards of the Africans cutting sugarcane. He took the pair of cards and tapped it on the triangle stone, then he flipped it over, and instead of the character cutting cane, they were standing jubilant in the ocean.

"Now that character is free," Kyle said. "You're trying to free everybody."

"And what are you trying to do?" I asked.

"I'm trying to free my characters and stop you from getting yours all free," he said.

Kyle organized the double-sided cards. He set several of them to his left on the table. "These are my seventeenth-century characters and stuff." He set a smaller group of cards to his right on the table. "These are my present-day characters," he said. Finally, he set the card with the triangle stone in the center.

"We each pull from our deck to make things happen," Kyle said. "I can play a card in one of my worlds to move things forward, or in one of my opponent's worlds to block."

"Okay," I said. "Got it. I think."

"Watch and learn," Kyle said.

"Are we gonna play a game?" I asked.

"Sorry," he said. "I'm about to play with someone online. We play what's called virtual/mix, where you each have your own decks IRL and you play via video chat."

"Cool," I said. "Okay if I watch?"

"Sure," he said.

For the first ten minutes, I watched him arranging the rest of his cards, the ones with the gold "Triángulo" on the back. He was picking from a large set of piles and arranging a deck.

This deck-building went on for fifteen minutes. Spy work is sometimes boring, but this was the worst. Like watching someone dust books in a library, dusting one book at a time and deciding which one to dust next.

Finally, he was ready. He messaged his friend and set up the video.

The opponent was a white kid in his late teens. His face was pale in the glow of the computer screen. He had a board in front of him, too. But I couldn't quite see the images.

"I have a trainee," Kyle said, and introduced the guy to me as Bret.

We waved at each other through the screen.

Kyle and Bret each held the cards in front of them, fanned out, with the backs to the screen that just had the gold triangle and the word "Triángulo." When they went to play a card, they turned it around to face the screen.

I had a hard time following it all, but in the seventeenth century, there were folks trying to get free, with slave catchers chasing them, a Maroon colony to protect, and initiations to perform. In the present time, there were superpowers you needed to build and superpowers you needed to block. I was trying to see if Kyle was playing particularly hard on the side of the enslavers, but I was too new to the game to really tell.

About an hour later, Kyle had just played a major card and was gloating with victory as Bret shuffled frantically through his hand to respond.

"I think that's the game, Bret," Kyle said. "Unless you have something very unexpected."

Bret looked from his deck to his screen. "Maybe I do," he said. "Maybe I'm just letting you win so you can look good in front of your new trainee."

"Keep telling yourself that, Bret," Kyle said with a smirk.

The two of them signed off.

"That was a short game I just won," Kyle said. "We played with fewer cards, because Bret has to go to work soon."

"Wow," I said. "Maybe we could play sometime."

"I guess," he said. "I have a friend I usually play with, but he's working today."

"Cool," I said. "Maybe I could watch the two of you in real life. It was hard to see what was going on through the screen."

"Sure," he said. "I owe you one for letting me borrow the comic book. I gotta go do homework. See you at school?"

I nodded.

He got up and left a plate covered with crumbs, an empty cup, and the open board with several wet rings on it.

I tidied everything so that the Latina barista wouldn't have to deal with it. Kyle obviously didn't care about leaving a mess for her—but did it mean he had racist tendencies that I would have to watch for, or was he just being an ordinary oblivious teenage guy? I felt like I was no closer to having an answer.

TWELVE

In English class, Ms. Bellman passed out a sheet on decoding Shakespeare. When was I ever going to need to know the word "forsooth"? Why were these stories so important that we had to slog through all the Elizabethan English we couldn't understand, but people thought it was "too hard" to read a present-day novel with a few Spanish words in it?

Before we got started, Kyle turned and handed me back the comic.

"I looked up the Triángulo game online last night," I whispered. "I learned some cool stuff. Can we talk at lunch?"

"Sure," he said with a shrug.

Our teacher shushed us, and we got back to work.

As we walked over to the cafeteria, I started into the speech I'd rehearsed.

"So I was looking online, and it seems like there are a lot of different strategies," I said.

"Yeah," Kyle said. "Of course, the obvious one is to get the best cards you can."

"Right," I said. "But it's so weird. I mean, you're sort of playing two games at once. Where you're the supposed 'good guy' in your game, but the supposed 'bad guy' in your opponent's game. It sort of makes the idea of good and bad . . . like . . . meaningless."

Kyle shrugged. "Like how?" We walked into the cafeteria and stood in the line.

"I mean," I said carefully. "The whole idea of good and bad is sort of relative, right?"

"In the game?" he said. "Yeah. You want bad things to happen to your opponent, but not your side. Ugh. Chicken potpie. Speaking of bad things happening to you."

"What about the Devil's Advocate strategy?" I asked. "It seems like that would be one way to really catch your opponent by surprise." I took a plastic tray from the stack. "Unless you just played that way all the time."

"I've definitely heard of people who do that," Kyle said.

"Do . . . do they do it just as a strategy?" I asked. "Or

do they maybe really . . . sort of sympathize with those characters?"

"I mean," Kyle said. "That's what I like about the comic books and the graphic novels. Naturalezo isn't a one-dimensional villain. You really get to see how hard things were for him, you know? You get to see how he got the way he is."

I could feel my pulse quicken. He was feeling sympathy for the enslaver's side?

We walked over to the same table we'd sat at before. He didn't say hello to anyone else there. They all seemed to be reading. Maybe it was the bookworm table.

"Yeah," I said. "I noticed that, too. He was raised to expect a certain type of lifestyle. To expect that he would inherit this huge estate and all this wealth. His whole family had led him to expect it. He wasn't just going to let it go because . . . because the slaves decided to rebel."

"*Enslaved people*," Kyle corrected. "My friend has been reminding me to say 'enslaved people.' He told me that saying 'slave' is sort of racist."

What? The son of a white supremacist was calling *me* racist? I stammered for what to say. "How do you mean?" I asked.

"He said that no one was really a slave," Kyle said. "That it, like, puts the problem on them. That they were people who were kidnapped and forced to work. If you say 'enslaved people,' it sort of more puts the blame on the enslavers, I guess."

"Your friend is Black?" I asked. I couldn't quite picture him with a Black friend.

"No," he said. "Latino. Or Latinx? I can't quite keep up with all the name changes."

I was so rattled that I almost said "Latine," which is what my family used, since we traveled internationally, and the *x* in "Latinx" was hard for some Spanish-speakers to pronounce.

"I'm trying to be more woke, you know?" he said.

"Uh, yeah," I said. "Thanks. I'll . . . I'll try to be more . . . woke . . . too."

I didn't know what to say after that, so I just dug into my chicken potpie, giving it much more attention than it deserved.

I skipped my PE class and went into the girls' bathroom. Standing in one of the stalls, I texted Mom and told her what I'd learned.

"Remember the assignment," she texted back. "It's good that Kyle doesn't seem to share his dad's values. You'll be safer that way. He's still our best lead to find John Summer."

"So I should still go to the café to try to play Triángulo with him?" I wrote back.

"Definitely," she replied.

"Let's move it, ladies!" an adult voice came into the girls' bathroom. "Time to get to class."

I signed off in a final text and flushed the toilet I hadn't used. I made a show of giving my hands a quick wash in front of the security guard before I hustled out of the restroom.

The bell rang, and students streamed into the hallway from all directions. I almost missed Kyle in the crush, but fortunately, he was tall.

"Hey," I said. "Glad I ran into you. Are you playing Triángulo again today?"

"Yeah," he said.

"Can I join you again?"

"Sure," he said. I could never tell with Kyle if I was welcome or not. But I was a spy, not someone really trying to make friends. So I was going to take anything but a no as a yes.

"Okay," I said. "See you at the café."

"Hey, Kyle," a voice came from behind me. "Who are you inviting to join our game without telling me?"

I turned around and saw the cute Latino boy that I had noticed in the library standing there, smiling. He had dark curly hair, rich brown skin, and slanted eyes, and I felt a little jump of excitement in my chest.

"Oh," Kyle said. "Her name is ANN-drea. This is my friend Ramón."

We nodded hello.

"Kyle didn't exactly invite me," I said. "I more invited myself along."

Ramón laughed. "I heard you were the newest freshman with the First-Class girls. You wanna play Triángulo? That's hilarious. See you at the café."

Then he took off down the hall in the opposite direction.

"So that's your woke friend?" I asked.

Kyle nodded.

My eyes followed Ramón. This assignment was definitely looking up.

THIRTEEN

Carson was a low-slung town. Most of the buildings were one or two stories. Mostly stucco, but some brick. Many had red tile roofs, and downtown they had those upright faces like in Western movies. If it weren't for the cars, you might expect two gunslingers to face off in the middle of downtown.

After school, I went to the post office to pick up a general delivery package. Jerrold had arranged for these particular comic books to be express mailed from the East Coast.

The post office was in one of those buildings with the Western-town facade. It had a bank of mailboxes and a black-and-white-checkered linoleum floor. I stood in line for five minutes, listening to a stressed mom toggle back and forth between keeping her kids from tearing up the post office and talking to her dad on the phone about how to fix his computer. Finally, she finished her business and it was my turn. A middle-aged clerk with starched hair and a lot of mascara verified my ID and gave me a package.

She checked my ID: Andrea Burke.

"Here you go, hon," she said.

I leaned against the counter and called my mom.

"Sí," I said. "El paquete llegó." I caught myself. "The package arrived just fine."

"That's swell, dear," Mom said.

I laughed. "Adiós," I said. "I mean, bye."

I turned around and ran into Ramón, who was staring at me, openmouthed.

"You speak Spanish?" he asked.

"Yeah—uh—" I stammered. "I was talking to my—my old nanny."

"She must have been a great nanny. You've got a good accent."

"Yeah," I said, trying to recall what I had said. Had I given anything away? I had just talked about the package, right? "I'm trying to speak to her in English now. She's trying to learn."

"Good for you," he said. "You still coming to the café?"

"Yep! See you soon!" I tossed over my shoulder as I fled from the post office.

I hustled down the street and didn't slow down till I had turned the corner and I was out of Ramón's sight.

I found myself standing in front of the eyebrow place, and I wondered again about my brows. Ramón had thick eyebrows, too. It looked normal to me.

Soon after Kyle, Ramón, and I met at the café, it became clear that Ramón was the more experienced player. Kyle got up to buy another pack of cards, and Ramón shook his head. "That's how they get you," he said. "American players think more merchandise makes you better."

"So I take it you won't be buying a custom board like Kyle?" I asked.

Ramón shook his head. "A waste of money."

"Don't yuck my yum," Kyle said, and he set his new deck on the table before grabbing the board from the game shelf.

"So Kyle was teaching you yesterday?" Ramón asked.

I nodded and he gave a short bark of a laugh. "I'm sure he's loving being the experienced one."

"Ramón thinks that just because he *introduced* me to the game that he'll always be the more experienced one," Kyle said. "But I'm the one that's put in way more time playing online than him."

"Yet I've consistently beat you when we play at home," Ramón said.

At home? Wait. The FBI file said that Kyle and his mom lived with a nanny, but I'd assumed that was out-of-date. Was Ramón the son of the nanny?

Kyle opened the pack and flipped quickly through it.

"Get anything good?" Ramón asked.

Kyle shook his head. "Nothing I didn't already have," he said.

Ramón raised an eyebrow at me, like, *See? I told you it was a waste of money.*

They started playing, explaining to me as they went. The game was fast-paced, but I was starting to get the hang of it. I was especially enjoying the way they quipped back and forth as they played. My mom calls it trash talking.

The two of them had been playing for half an hour when we were interrupted.

"Kyle!" a voice called from the door of the café. It belonged to a frazzled woman with pale hair and a clanging key ring in her hand.

"I'm double-parked," she said, rushing up to the table. She gave Ramón and me a distracted wave. We waved back.

"Mom?" Kyle said. "What are you doing here?"

"You have to meet with that math tutor," Kyle's mom said, picking up his backpack off the back of the chair. "How could you forget? We're going to be late. I've been texting you."

"I forgot that was today," he said, gathering his cards. "Sorry." He turned to me. "ANN-drea, you're my witness that I was winning."

"Oh dear God, just come on," his mom said.

Kyle didn't hurry, but he finished gathering his cards and followed his mom out the door.

After they had left, I turned to Ramón. "Is he gonna be in trouble?"

Ramón rolled his eyes. "That was just Kyle pulling a Kyle."

"What do you mean?" I asked.

"Kyle does what Kyle wants to do," Ramón said. "If he wanted to get tutored, he'd have been ready. But when he doesn't want to do something, he sabotages it."

"He doesn't want to do better in math?" I asked.

"He doesn't care much about grades," Ramón said. "He'd rather sit around after school and play video games."

"I thought he liked coming to the café," I said.

"He likes it now," Ramón said, shaking his head. "But when he's at home, he's a total couch potato. If he could get his grades up, it would cut down on the arguing between him and his mom."

"They fight a lot?" I asked.

"All the time," he said. "And we live together. Our moms are housemates. I hear every little squabble."

Housemates?

"I'm not sure why his mom is on his case so bad," Ramón went on. "She wants him to go to college, so he can get a good job eventually, but she makes plenty of money. Kyle could live in his bedroom for the rest of his life and still just work a few short shifts a week like he does now. My mom doesn't make as much money and really needs my salary. I'll definitely need to be going to college and getting a good job. You probably wouldn't know about that." He didn't say it in a mean way, but I still bristled. "I heard you went to private school, right? Have you ever had a job?"

"No," I said. ANN-drea Burke had never had a job. I certainly couldn't tell him, *I'm working right now.*

"But, hey," I asked, "could I take his place? Playing Triángulo?"

"Do you have a deck?" he asked.

I shook my head.

"You can buy a starter deck," he suggested. "Too bad Kyle took his character deck, or we could have saved you some money."

"Can we save even more by playing with bottle caps and rocks?" I asked, remembering what Kyle had said.

"Nah," he said. "They scratch the finish on the board."

"Okay," I said. I went to the register and bought both decks.

The character decks were all the same. Two-sided cards, each showing a character or a place. The plantation. The Maroon colony. Different enslaved people. There was a seventeenth-century Olumide, Arantxa, and BaguaNi, as well as a set of the three heroes in present day. There was a seventeenth-century villain, Naturalezo, and a contemporary version. On one side of each card was a drawing of the character in muted earth tones, and on the other side, the character was in bold and brilliant color.

"Wait—I thought the seventeenth-century Arantxa was really rare!" I said. "Isn't this worth, like, a thousand dollars?"

"That's the Arantxa action card," Ramón explained. "The character deck is different. You don't use them to make plays—they're just pieces you move around the board, like the hat, the car, or the shoe in Monopoly."

"Ugh, this is confusing," I complained, but as he kept explaining, I started to get it.

We each had a deck of sixty cards—three times what Kyle had used with Bret—plus characters. As we played, I learned basic moves, like using Initiation and Transformation cards to flip my heroes into the bright colors, which meant they had superpowers.

I tried a few different moves I thought would be smart, but he told me they weren't allowed.

"Isn't it a conflict of interest for you to be my teacher and my opponent?"

He laughed. "What? You don't trust me, Grasshopper?"

I smiled. "What if I play this card?" I asked, putting a blight on the sugarcane on his plantation.

"Whoa!" he said.

"You should be proud of me," I said. "You taught me everything I know."

"Maybe you're learning too fast," he said, playing a card to reduce the blight by half.

By the time he beat me, by starting a successful rebellion and defeating the villain in the present day, the sun was low on the horizon.

"Good game," he said.

"That's easy for you to say," I said. "You totally crushed me first time out. Isn't the teacher supposed to let the student win to boost her confidence?"

"This game isn't for the weak-willed," he said. He stood and stretched. "I'm hungry. Coffee drinks and cookies aren't doing it for me."

"Same here," I said. "Is there anything good to eat nearby?"

"There's some great pizza," he said. "But it's a bit of a walk. Do you need to be home soon?"

"Nah," I said. "My mom works late."

"Mine, too," he said. "Let's go, then."

"I should warn you," he said as we headed down the street. "The pizza place is sort of . . . in transition. They used to be a regular place that just sold good pizza. But now they have all sorts of fancy toppings. Goat cheese. Heirloom tomatoes. Olives brined in barley salt."

"What's barley salt?" I asked.

"Nobody knows," Ramón said. "But it's really expensive."

I laughed.

We had only walked three blocks before the businesses ended and it was all residential. The houses were small and low. There were lots of churches and the occasional corner store.

"I had no idea Triángulo was a game and not just a comic book," I said. I called it "Try-ANG-you-low" instead of "Tree-AHN-goo-lo" with the Spanish hard *r*.

"For years only the Arantxa comics crossed over," he said.

"Crossed over what?" I asked.

"From Latin America," he said. "Arantxa has only been major in the US since the push for more female superheroes a few years ago."

He "explained" a bunch more to me that I already knew from my Wikipedia deep dive. I pretended that I was hearing it for the first time, saying things like "Really?" and "Cool, I didn't know that." He told me a few things I hadn't heard, like that the first printing of the Arantxa card is priceless, and you can recognize it because there's a typo in the map of the Basque Country.

It was still light out, and I wasn't used to seeing so much sky. The low buildings meant that a cloudless blue stretched above us in the widest arc I'd ever seen anywhere but the beach. Finally, we got to a small cluster of businesses, including a vintage clothing store and a pet groomer.

Every now and then, Ramón would mention my name. Like when we got to the pizza place and he turned to me: "ANN-drea, what do you like on your pizza?"

What I wanted was to correct his pronunciation, so I could hear him say my name the right way: ahn-DRAY-ah, with that Spanish *r*.

Instead, I said, "Pepperoni."

He smiled and ordered the same.

We sat down on the hard plastic seats. I realized that we hadn't mentioned Kyle in hours. I hadn't even thought about him. *Kyle* was my assignment. Not Ramón. Although Ramón was his friend. And his roommate. So it made sense that I was out having pizza with Ramón. It made sense that I was looking across the table into his long-lashed brown eyes. I broke eye contact and stared out the plate-glass window onto the quiet street. On the other side was an old-timey barbershop.

"How long have you and Kyle been roommates?" I asked.

"Since we were babies. I was two and he was one," Ramón said. "When his dad split, my mom was Kyle's nanny. Then we got evicted, and our moms left Phoenix and moved in together. They figured it would save on rent and childcare. We've been living in Carson ever since."

"You guys are like brothers," I said.

"Kyle is like an annoying little brother," he said.

I missed my own brother, but of course I couldn't say anything. There would be no way to explain it without blowing my cover.

"Me being a year older doesn't seem like that much now, but it used to. Don't get me wrong. Kyle is okay. But we're close in that way when you care about someone because they're family. Not like a friend that's so close he's like a brother, you know? I had a friend like that, and it was different."

"What do you mean 'had'?" I asked.

"His name was Miguel," Ramón said. "We were tight from kindergarten through middle school." He looked down at the last bit of his pizza. "He was definitely my best friend. But then . . . he moved away."

I could tell that there was more to the story, but I didn't want to pry. "Did you stay in touch?" I asked.

"For a while," Ramón said. "He was actually the one who got me started playing Triángulo. It was everywhere in Mexico."

"Is that where he lives now?" I asked.

He looked down again. "His dad was deported. The rest of them were born here, but . . . they couldn't afford to stay." He cleared his throat. "Anyway, we played online for a while, but then the family lost their internet access. We haven't really talked since. I wrote him a couple of letters, but I haven't heard back."

I nodded. I didn't know what to say. "I'm sorry," I said. "That you—that your friend's family got deported."

"Yeah, but part of me was jealous," he said. "His dad got deported, but his family was able to stay together. We couldn't follow my dad."

"Where did he go?" I asked.

He shook his head. "He died."

Ugh. How was I asking these questions that kept leading to these really awful answers? "I'm sorry," I said again, but it sounded sort of pathetic.

He shook his head. "Died when I was a baby. I don't even remember him. Just a picture. How about you?"

"My dad had a midlife crisis," I said. "Divorced my mom and went to find himself."

"Like Kyle's dad," Ramón said.

My ears perked up. "He had a midlife crisis?" I asked.

"From what I hear, it was more like a responsibility crisis," he said. "He's Mr. Outdoorsy. He had all these visions of going fishing and hunting and hiking with his son. Well, you don't get to do that with a newborn baby. He didn't wait for Kyle to get big enough."

"Some parents act like kids are accessories," I said.

"Kyle's such a couch potato now," Ramón said. "The opposite of his dad's dreams for him."

"His dad sounds like a jerk," I said.

"White guys," Ramón said. "It's like, 'Gotta be my way all the time.'"

"Was his dad really . . . I don't know . . . all about being white or something?" I wasn't sure how to get Ramón to say more about John Summer.

"Not that I know of," Ramón said. "I just meant in general."

I nodded and finished my pizza. "This was so good," I said. "Next time let's get the barley salt."

He laughed. "Just so long as we don't get the weird crust."

I laughed, too, then stood up. "I'm gonna get some water," I said. "Want some?"

"Sure," he said.

I swear, I wasn't gone for more than a minute—just like four steps across the floor to the water spigot and the time it took to fill the two cups—but when I got back, he was finishing a drawing of me on a napkin in blue ballpoint pen.

It was startling how much it looked like me. The pen strokes were simple and fast, but he totally captured all the important lines of my features. Sort of like those caricatures that people draw at street fairs, but the head wasn't oversized.

On the one hand, it was amazing because he had done it so fast. But on the other hand, it was bittersweet because the picture definitely looked like a white girl.

I mustered a big smile. "Wow!" I said. "How did you do that so fast?"

"I've always been good at drawing quickly," he said. "That's my superpower."

"Can I keep it?" I asked.

"Of course," he said, then he looked at his phone. "It's late. I should walk you home."

I wanted to tell him that I was trained in five different martial arts and carried a knife, but it was too cute that he thought he could protect me. "You don't need to do that," I said.

"My mom taught me to be a gentleman and never to let my female friends walk home alone."

"So we're friends?" I asked. "You've forgiven my shady past with the First-Class Cabin girls?"

"We're friends," he said. "If you want to be. I mean, in addition to you being my Triángulo trainee."

"Friends," I agreed. We walked out the door of the pizza place, and our shoulders brushed against each other. I felt a jolt of energy.

Kyle, I reminded myself. *Kyle is your assignment.*

On the way home, in the gathering dusk, Ramón was like a tour guide pointing out the neighborhood that was changing. It used to be mostly Mexican but was now much whiter.

When we got to my house, he playfully punched my shoulder. "Not bad for your first day at Triángulo, Grasshopper. I'm proud of you."

"I'll study up for tomorrow," I said.

He turned to go. "See you at school," he said.

When I walked inside, I reported everything I'd learned about Kyle to Mom. "One other thing," I asked. "Why would someone call someone else 'Grasshopper'?"

"It's from an old eighties movie, *The Karate Kid*," she said. "It's what the master called the boy he's training. Why?"

"Someone at school said it," I told her. "One of the girls." I wasn't ready to tell her about Ramón just yet.

FOURTEEN

The next day after English class, Kyle just fell into step beside me, and we walked over to the cafeteria for lunch. The line was unusually short, and we sat down right away.

As he began to wolf down his lunch, Kyle pulled out a BaguaNi comic book. BaguaNi was the Taino Bohique in the Triángulo origin story. In the contemporary superhero series, he had the power of water. He could breathe beneath the sea, and the pressure never affected him. Also, sea creatures saw him as a friend, ally, and protector.

I had been reading about the Indigenous Taino culture that he represented. My mom said she'd had an uncle who'd told her they had Taino heritage. Her grandmother had denied it, and the uncle had died before Mom could ask more questions. It was weird to read about Taino culture and not really know if it was my heritage or not. I wished that I had more access to that part of my past.

So when I saw that Kyle was reading the BaguaNi series of the Triángulo universe, I got excited. But reading over his shoulder, I was soon disappointed. In the comic book Kyle was reading—some sort of spin-off from the main series, it seemed—BaguaNi had been bewitched by a group of mermaids into living in an undersea cave with them. BaguaNi was sitting on a treasure chest with a crown tilted at a rakish angle. Surrounding him were mermaids of all colors with shell bikini tops and flowing hair.

I rolled my eyes. "You're scraping the bottom of the Triángulo barrels."

"Tell me about it," Kyle said. "There's no action, and the mermaids just fight over him."

"It looks like some kind of cheesy music video," I said.

"But it's the only new comic that's come out," Kyle said.

"Or is it?" I asked, then lifted up the latest graphic novel Jerrold had sent.

"First dibs!" Kyle yelled. He was already pushing aside his tray and opening the book.

The lunch bell rang.

"Can I hang on to this?" Kyle asked.

"Sure," I said. "You can give it back to me at the café after school."

Kyle nodded absently. He was so caught up in the book that he was totally oblivious to everyone filing out of the lunchroom.

"See you at the café, Kyle," I said. "And don't forget to go to class."

I ran into Ramón in the hallway between my next two classes.

"Hey, I hope you've been studying," Ramón said. "Triángulo, I mean."

"Definitely," I said. "I was online until late. Watching videos. Lurking on message boards where people were arguing. Planning my cosplay outfit."

He laughed out loud. "Don't tell me. You're going as Arantxa?"

"Too predictable," I said. "I'm going as the villain, Naturalezo."

He tilted his head to the side. "I can sort of see it. You could do the sinister thing."

"Excuse me?" I said.

"Not that you're a sinister person," he said. "Just that you could pull it off. Some people can't. They lack the depth."

I gave him the side-eye. "Good save," I said.

"See you at the café," he said, and headed into his class.

When I got to the café, I went to our usual table, but there was no one there. I sat down, feeling a little forlorn with my starter deck.

I got some tea and a cupcake. I peeled off the paper and ate it slowly, picking off chunks from the bottom up. I always eat the top last so that I can savor the frosting.

Ten minutes later, Ramón came to the door. I smiled at him, but he wasn't alone. He was with a girl our age—Latina, with copper skin, darkly lined eyes, and glossy black hair. They were speaking Spanish. A lump formed in my throat.

It's just work, I told myself. *Don't be unprofessional.*

But I had an unprofessional pang in my chest when he gave her a warm hug goodbye. She walked away with a bouncy step.

I dragged my eyes away from her and looked down at my deck of cards as Ramón walked across the café toward the back.

"Oh, hey," Ramón said. "I didn't realize you were here, or I would have introduced you."

"That's okay," I said.

"I'm sure you'll meet her eventually," he said. "She's my favorite cousin, Sara."

Cousin! The tension in my throat and chest melted. "I look forward to it," I said. "Where's Kyle?"

"At the orthodontist," Ramón said. "His mom came

to pick him up from school. He texted me that he'd give you your book tomorrow."

Kyle wasn't coming? I was disappointed for the operation, but also kind of excited to have more time with Ramón. "Thanks for letting me know," I said. "Am I ever going to see that book again?"

"Definitely," he said. "I'll make sure."

We played the game for the next two hours. I did better this time. I poisoned the water in the enslaver's well. I sank the ship that came to collect the sugarcane. I got nearly all my freed Africans to the Maroon colony. But Ramón did everything faster, and when he flipped the game to the present, I didn't have any good cards left and he won again.

We stood up from the table. The foot I'd tucked under me had fallen asleep.

When we hit the door, there was a line on the street.

"Are all these people coming to play Triángulo?" I asked.

Ramón laughed. "No way. These guys came for Magic: The Gathering. Triángulo is just starting here in Carson."

Several of the teen boys wore dark cloaks with their hoods up. "Remind me not to cross these guys," I said.

"They're pretty harmless," he said. "You want pizza again?"

"Sure," I said, trying not to feel too excited that he wanted to have dinner together a second time.

We walked across town by a different route. We passed a Salvadoran restaurant that had plátanos. I would definitely be telling Mom about it.

"This part over here, they call 'the hood,'" Ramón said. "When white people moved into that other neighborhood, the brown people all moved to this area."

I laughed. It looked mostly the same as the rest of the town. In between the low stucco houses, there were more two-story apartment buildings with exterior walkways. No trash on the street. No one yelling on their porches. No cars screeching by. No loud music.

"I know, right?" Ramón said. "Being from LA, this has got to look like a hick town."

"Not so much that," I said. "It just looks really quiet around here. Hardly 'the hood.'"

"Basically, this is where the Mexican and Central American folks live," he said. "I wanted you to see it for yourself before people started saying to beware of this side of town. It's no big deal."

We walked past a corner store playing cumbia, where a mother walked out with three laughing little girls in dresses and flip-flops.

At the pizza place, we ordered what I already thought of as our usual and sat down.

Once again, I stared out the window, avoiding Ramón's high cheekbones and the twisted tooth that flashed when he smiled or pronounced the letter *e*.

Then suddenly, I blinked in disbelief: What? The First-Class girls were coming in? For pizza?

". . . so amazing and I heard it's cauliflower and flaxseed-meal flour, so it's fiber and not carbs," Mandy was saying as they opened the door and a bell tinkled their arrival.

"Danger," I murmured to Ramón. "Pastel invasion at eleven o'clock."

He laughed and nearly spit out his soda.

"Are you trying to kill me?" he asked as he struggled to swallow.

I was about to make a snappy retort when Mandy and the crew noticed us.

"I'm surprised to see you here," one girl said.

"Yeah," said Mandy. She eyed Ramón. "Shouldn't you be at the taco truck instead?"

Before I could stop myself, I said, "That's racist."

I was blowing my cover. I was supposed to be white. Supposed to be setting myself up to connect with the son of a white supremacist. But instead, I was hanging out with the Latino guy and calling out the white girls?

"What did you say?" Mandy asked.

"She called you racist," her friend said.

"Just forget it," I said.

"Let's go," Mandy said. "I've lost my appetite. And it looks like they're out of flax pizza, anyway."

They left in a huff, and I turned to Ramón.

"You know," he said. "You don't need to try and

score cool points with me by talking about race. I can defend myself. I don't need a white girl to come to my rescue."

"I'm not—I'm not trying to rescue you. You don't have to be a person of color to find racism offensive."

He shrugged. "That's true."

I finished my pizza. "Let's go," I said. I brushed pizza-crust crumbs from my hands and stood up.

Outside, we walked in an awkward silence. The last rays of the sunset were visible at the tops of the hills to the west of the town.

"You don't need to walk me," I said. "It's not as late tonight."

"I want to," he said. "Not just because it's the gentlemanly thing to do, but because I like . . . talking to you."

"Okay, then say something," I said, laughing a little.

"How about those Wildcats?" he said.

"Those what?" I asked.

"Basketball," he said, laughing.

"I don't follow sports," I said.

"Me neither," he said. "I'm more of the nerdy type."

"Really?" I said. "You don't seem nerdy to me. Kyle maybe, but not you."

"Well, I am," he said. "And there's one thing you should know about us nerds."

"What's that?" I asked as we turned down the corner onto my block.

"It's been sort of a boys' club until recently," he said.

"Okay," I said. "Then thanks for letting girls in the club."

He laughed. "No, I just mean . . . we're not . . . I'm not used to having girls around. Girls as friends. Girls as—"

I cut him off. "Looks like my mom's home," I said, gazing up at my brightly lit fake house. "I'm glad you think of me as a friend," I said. "It can be hard to make friends as the new kid."

I could tell he wanted to say something personal to me. And I didn't want to hear it.

I mean, I did. Wow, I seriously did. With those big brown eyes and long lashes and cute smile. But I had a job to do. Ramón wasn't the one whose father was trying to kill people. Ramón wasn't the one whose confidence I needed to gain. I didn't have to date Kyle, but I wasn't sure how he'd feel about me dating his friend, and I didn't want to risk finding out.

"ANN-drea—"

"I should go," I said. "See you tomorrow."

"Tomorrow's Saturday," he said.

"I know," I said. But I had forgotten. He had me flustered. "I meant, I'll see you at the café. Triángulo is really fun. I might hang out there all weekend."

"I work Saturday in the electronics store at the mall," Ramón said. "Kyle's got a shift, too. And Sunday's the weekly tournament. Mostly you can't get in if you're not a player."

"Maybe I'll play," I said. "You saw yourself that I'm getting better."

"Play with who?" Ramón asked. "It's partners."

"Partners?" I asked.

"Yeah," he said. "Me and Kyle are signed up. If you want to join, you need someone to play with."

"Good to know," I said.

"ANN-drea, if you could wait just a minute, I—"

My text alert sounded.

"It's my mom," I said. "So if I don't see you Sunday, I'll see you Monday at school."

"ANN-drea—"

I turned and fled up the stairs.

FiFTEEN

I had my key out by the time I got to the top of the wooden porch. I stood between the cheerful pots of pink and red flowers that the great-aunt had hanging on either side of her door. I unlocked it as fast as I could, went inside, and closed it quickly behind me.

Mom was walking into the living room with a plate of grilled cheese sandwiches and creamed spinach. Wow, she never ate foods like that at home. Even her dinner was part of her cover.

"How'd it go?" she asked.

"Are you asking as a mom or a colleague?" I asked.

She laughed. "Both. Let me return to the protocol. Anything time-sensitive?"

"Yeah," I said. "I have to report to Jerrold. Then we can check in."

I typed up a quick report to Jerrold, telling him that Kyle's dad had a love for nature, and that I likely wouldn't see him for the next two days because he was working on Saturday and I didn't have a partner for the tournament on Sunday.

I wanted to say something about Ramón, but I didn't dare. Impulsively, I dug in my binder pocket for the napkin drawing he had made of me at the pizza place. I slipped upstairs and taped it to the wall next to my bed. I positioned it low, in the corner, so the white of the napkin blended in with the white of the pillow and fluffy comforter. Perfect. I would just need to move it before Mom changed the sheets and did the laundry.

Back down in the living room, Mom was eating peanut butter cookies and monitoring several white supremacist websites.

"Is it difficult to read that stuff?" I asked.

"I reward myself with the cookies," she said.

"I need to confess something," I said. "I accidentally read the word 'purity' on one of those websites. I obviously need a reward, too."

She laughed as I took a cookie.

"How did it go?" she asked as she slid the laptop aside.

I told her about the orthodontist appointment,

the info on Kyle's dad, and the tournament. I told her about the taco truck comment and how I had to clean it up. She said I did a good job on that one. Mom was always so supportive, and I wanted to tell her about my crush on Ramón, but I just . . . couldn't. I didn't want to seem unprofessional. I didn't want to let her and everyone down. I needed a friend to tell about it, not my mother and coworker. But a friend was the one thing I didn't have.

"Open that laptop," I said. "Let me read another word so I can have another cookie."

She handed me the last one. "No need for you to read any more of this," she said. "You already deserve the reward."

If we kept eating peanut butter cookies while reading about white supremacy, I wondered if we would develop a peanut allergy.

When I woke up in the morning, I had a message from Jerrold.

> Great work so far. Your assignment for the day is to search the house while everyone is at work. In particular:
> • Search computer to see if there's been any contact between Kyle and his dad.
> • Search photos to see if you can find a clearer picture of John Summer—so far,

we only have the license photo and the
video clip, but if we can find more, they'll be
able to do a wider search of mug shots and
see if he's been operating elsewhere under
an alias.

I rode over on my skateboard to the address Jerrold
had given me. The Factory had chosen a nearby HQ
for our operation; it was a ten-minute walk to Kyle's
house, so only a five-minute skateboard ride.

A pair of white-haired ladies walked by, wearing
athletic gear, swinging their arms with little barbells
in their hands. They smiled at me, and I smiled back.

When I got to the corner of the boys' block, I pulled
my hoodie over my head and skated past their house. A
yellow stucco cottage. No sounds coming from inside.
No sign of the boys. And best of all, no car in the
driveway.

The neighborhood was quiet. A few lawns had
sprinklers running. Mostly one- and two-story houses.
A couple low apartment buildings.

I skated to the corner and doubled back. Still no car
in the driveway.

I jumped off the board and passed by slowly,
looking through the living room window. No sign of
anyone. I walked onto the porch to ring the bell. Still
nobody.

I looked around behind me. The sidewalk was

empty. No one visible in any of the windows of the houses or apartments across the street.

I slipped over the side of the porch and crept up the driveway, rounding the back of the house. They had planted a beautiful food garden in the back. I didn't have time to stop and admire it, because I saw that the back window was open a crack.

I hid my skateboard behind a bush, picked my way through the rows of cucumber and corn, and stood under the window. It was too high to climb into. Fortunately, I had brought a booster for this. It was like a foldable tripod stool. I unfolded it, clipped it to my leg, and stood on it to boost myself up through the window. The stool dangled from my foot. Reaching to get it, I lost my balance and tumbled into the room, the stool crashing after me.

I froze where I landed. I dreaded hearing running footsteps and someone demanding to know what the hell I was doing here, but I heard only a car go by on the street and a kid in a nearby backyard calling her dog, the unfortunately named Gumdrop.

Slowly, I unfroze and unclipped the stool from my ankle, securing it around my waist.

The room I had tumbled into was a back sunporch that had been converted into a bedroom. There was a neatly made-up single bed, a small dresser, and a minidesk with a bookshelf. It was clearly a teenage boy's room, but which boy? The tidiness made me think of Ramón, but maybe Kyle's mom cleaned his room for him. There weren't any papers on the desk, and the books on the shelf didn't give much of a clue: textbooks, comic books, and sci-fi/fantasy novels. There was a whole Triángulo section, with comics and cards. I was hoping for a laptop, but I didn't see one.

I turned my attention to the chest of drawers. The top drawer was underwear. Ugh. I mean, it was clean, but I felt weird rummaging through either of these guys' underwear. Nothing interesting in there, so I moved on.

The second drawer was T-shirts. There was the Arantxa shirt Kyle had worn on the first day I met him. Yes! It was Kyle's room. I looked through the rest of the drawers and found only more clothes and a BaguaNi cosplay costume.

The small room didn't have a closet. I looked under the bed and found a shoebox. I opened it, and there were a bunch of baby pictures. Aha! I pulled out my phone, ready to snap copies of any pictures of John Summer, but upon closer look, I could see that the boy was brunette. Several photos were with a Latino man. One with two dark-haired parents. This must be Ramón as a baby, with *his* dad. Why would Kyle have Ramón's baby pictures?

Then it hit me. Kyle must have borrowed Ramón's

shirt. Wrong room. Dang. I closed the shoebox and slid it back under the bed.

Dusting off my hands, I reached for the double glass doors of the sunroom. They were wide, with several panes in each. I had just walked through and realized I was in the kitchen when I heard a car engine and the crunch of gravel under tires in the driveway.

I quickly closed the double doors and scrambled over to the window. I wouldn't be able to close it back the way it was when I came in, but that was better than getting caught. I scratched my arms a little as I climbed out and let my body drop to the ground.

I grabbed my skateboard and ran across the garden to the opposite side of the house from the driveway. There was a narrow strip between the side of the house and the neighbor's fence that was overgrown with weeds.

I crouched down in the walkway and crept toward the sidewalk.

When I heard the front door close, I turned and walked back toward the great-aunt's house, skateboard under my arm.

I thought I was home free, but at the end of the block, I ran into Kyle's mom carrying a pair of coffee cups. I didn't know what to say, so I kept walking.

"Excuse me," she called after I passed her. "Didn't I see you with Kyle and Ramón at the café? Did you come by looking for them?"

"Oh, yeah," I said, pretending I was just now recognizing her. "I didn't know you all lived here. I was just passing by. Don't they work today?"

She laughed. "Yes, thank God. I can finally get some spring cleaning done without two lumps on the couch."

"It's cool they can work together," I said.

"I'm glad they're expanding their social circle," she said. "I'm Emily."

"ANN-drea," I said.

She looked over my shoulder, back toward her house. "Alma! Come meet a friend of the boys!"

A slightly older version of the woman I'd seen in Ramón's photos came down their front steps and joined us. Kyle's mom introduced me to her. She had Ramón's same dark eyes.

"Nice to meet you, ANN-drea," Ramón's mom said with a smile. Her Spanish accent made me homesick.

They asked me a few questions. I said I was new in town and liked playing Triángulo with their sons.

We said our goodbyes, and as they walked away, I heard Kyle's mom say, "An actual girl? Can you believe it, Alma?"

At home, I messaged Jerrold:

No luck searching house. Both moms came home. Maybe next Sat.

He wrote back almost right away:

> Picked up some message board chatter that has us
> thinking there may be some communication soon
> between the terrorist and the weapon maker. I'm putting
> this operation on the front burner. We'll find a way to
> accelerate your friendship with Kyle. Stand by.

SIXTEEN

For the first half hour, I paced by the phone, waiting for whatever Jerrold had in mind. Mom told me that part of spycraft was patience. Don't burn out your adrenaline when nothing is happening. Take the downtime when you get it. But that was easier said than done.

I finally took her advice and sat down with her in the sunny living room. I had flipped over the puppy pillows, so it was just the curios in the cabinet that were watching me. Maybe I was getting used to it, or maybe I just didn't care because I was absorbed in the Triángulo comics.

I was reading Arantxa's origin story. She was a young Basque apprentice midwife being pursued by the

Spanish Inquisition. She cut off her hair and impersonated a Spanish soldier in order to escape to the New World, where she ended up on Caguama Island and hid in plain sight for a time. One night, however, she was drinking with the soldiers and wasn't tuned in to the signs that her period was coming. I turned the page to find out if she got caught, but Mom interrupted.

"How is this happening again?" she asked. "You get to read empowering feminist comics while I'm monitoring white supremacist websites?"

She had switched from peanut butter cookies to apple slices, because all the sweets were giving her a stomachache.

"A spy's duty is to serve," I said. "We each have our role to play."

Mom sucked her teeth. "Smartass," she muttered, and we laughed.

Half an hour later, just as Arantxa was closing in on Naturalezo's secret lair, there was a knock at the door.

We looked at each other. "Are you expecting anyone?" she asked.

"No," I said. I didn't know anyone in town, except the boys. And Mandy's crew. Jerrold was still in Los Angeles, wasn't he?

Mom put a gun in the back of her waistband and walked to the door.

Ramón did know where I lived. Maybe he had

gotten off work early. He didn't have my number. Maybe he would just stop by.

"Who is it?" Mom asked.

"Jerrold sent me," a female voice said.

Mom opened the door. Standing on the porch was a young Black woman with a stack of comic books.

"Who are you?" Mom asked.

"Reinforcements," she said, and walked in the door.

She was tall. Taller than my mom. Maybe taller than my dad, and full-figured, with pecan-brown skin. At first, her height made me think she was older, but when I got closer, I realized she was a teen, too. Maybe a year or so older than me.

She and Mom exchanged a classified set of passwords to identify each other. When they had each said the right things, we relaxed.

"I'm Imani Kennedy," she said, setting the comic books down on the blond wooden coffee table.

"ANN-drea Burke," I said.

"Barbara Burke," Mom said.

Imani squinted at us. "Are you Black?"

My mom laughed. "Depends how you measure," she said. "What gave it away?"

"You press your hair," Imani said.

"Is it obvious?" Mom asked, a hand flying to her temple.

"Only to trained spies with kinky hair."

Imani's hair was back in small cornrows that led up to a bun on top of her head.

"Are those your real names?" Imani asked.

"Let me put it this way," Mom said. "They gave us surnames that are much easier for the mainstream to pronounce."

"I'd have to guess you were either South Asian or Latinx," Imani said. "My money is on Latinx."

I opened my mouth but couldn't think what to say. Then suddenly, I burst into tears. It was overwhelming to have someone see the real me after so much pretending.

"Oh, honey," Mom said, and came to put her arms around me.

"Stop, Mami," I said, squirming away from her. "I mean, Mom. I'm trying to be professional."

"Girl," Imani said. "Don't suck it up when you don't have to. You're among fam. Just let it out."

And I did. I had a big cry on my mom's shoulder in front of a complete stranger. Not just any stranger, but my new partner, I guessed. I was so embarrassed.

Pulling myself together, I wiped my eyes and sat up.

"Sorry," I said.

"Don't be," Imani said. "You should have seen me on my first mission. I spent plenty of time crying with my mom. You really are mother and daughter, right?"

Mom nodded.

"Jerrold already briefed you about the mission?" I asked.

"Yep. I'm here to get you into that partners tournament this weekend," she said. "They were debating whether or not to send you a Black partner until you confirmed that Kyle doesn't seem to share his dad's beliefs. Besides, Jerrold said that time is of the essence."

"Have you played Triángulo before?" I asked.

"Only once," she said. "But I read a book about the game, along with a few of the comics, and I've been collecting cards, hoping to play again. There's a limited pool of people our age in the organization, so I guess that makes me the expert among the teen operatives. Plus, I was already in the region."

"Glad to have you on board," Mom said. "I've got to get back to monitoring white supremacy blogs." She gave a wry smile. "You know, the master race calls."

Imani laughed. "I'll remember that next time I get an assignment I don't like."

Imani and I sat down in the living room to get to know each other. She used to live in LA and actually had gone to Penfield Academy. I confirmed a few details of my cover story, and then she reached for the pile of books.

"Are we ready to get to it?" she asked. "These comic books aren't going to read themselves."

"It's a tough job," I said. "But I do it for my people."

After an hour of research, Mom ordered lunch for all of us.

"We should go to the café and practice the game," I said, and took a bite out of a crispy chicken taco.

"Sounds good," Imani said. "Is our cover that we're already friends?"

"Definitely not," I said. "Supposedly I just moved here and don't know anyone."

"I'm supposed to be homeschooled from a big family with lots of cousins," Imani said. "The story is that I'm just getting more privileges to go out."

"Sounds good," Mom said. "You two would naturally find each other and strike up a fast friendship."

"Okay," I said. "One of us should head over to the café now and try to get a table. Then the other one can come a little later. What do you think?"

"Sounds good," Imani said. "I should be the one to go."

"You sure?" I asked.

"Definitely," she said. "The big, tall Black girl has a much better chance of holding the table on her own."

"Real talk," Mom said.

"You should have a couple more tacos," I said. "The food at the café leaves a lot to be desired."

"You don't have to tell me twice," Imani said, and finished what was on her plate.

Less than an hour later, I walked into the café. The place was full. Imani was at a table in the back, arranging her Triángulo cards.

"Mind if I sit here?" I asked. Kyle and Ramón weren't around, but I wasn't sure if anyone here knew them, so the safest thing to do was to play our parts.

"It's cool," she said with a shrug. Dang. If I hadn't known she was expecting me, I would have assumed she really didn't want me to sit. She had the I-don't-care sullen teen thing down.

I pulled out my Triángulo deck and flipped through it.

"You play?" she asked.

"I'm just learning," I said.

"They have a tournament here, you know," she said.

"Tomorrow, right?" I asked. "I wanted to try, but I heard it's partners."

"Pretty bold," she said. "Trying to enter as a novice."

"How else do you learn?" I asked.

"You don't know a lot about the culture," she said. "When you enter a tournament, you want to be able to win at least one round. You want to be someone who other people want on their teams."

"How are you supposed to get good if you can't enter?" I asked.

"People get friends to teach them," Imani said.

"My friends who play are at work today," I said. "Seems like there's not that much time after school, and we can only finish one game."

Imani shrugged and looked at the counter. "I'm about to order another apple cider. If you want to learn, we could play."

"Sure," I said. "That'd be great. How's the cider?"

"Good," she said. "Coffee makes me jumpy. But you need to get something more expensive than water if you don't want the table bussers to start giving you dirty looks after the first hour."

"If you're gonna teach me, I'll treat," I said.

"Yeah, okay," she said, looking toward the door.

I got up to get the drinks. Wow, she did cool and detached so well. I seriously needed to take lessons from her.

Ramón had taught me to play with just sixty cards. But for a tournament, you played with one hundred cards each. I had to buy a few new packs.

After we'd settled into the game, I got off to a strong start in the seventeenth century, sending reinforcements from Spain to quell her slave rebellion. But she drew a Time Travel card and sent the game back to present day.

"Bam!" she said. "Take that!"

"No!" I said. "You knew I was weak in the present."

Once we shifted to the present, we each had to use our Arantxa, Olumide, and BaguaNi superhero cards to battle modern bad guys as well as Naturalezo, their nemesis from the past.

I tried to defend myself, but she had the cards to leach the superpowers from my villain and get her superheroes to full power. I played another Time Travel card in desperation, hoping that I could regain my footing in the seventeenth century, but she had a card that blocked it and kept us in the present.

I was so mad, I almost cussed in Spanish. "Dang!" I said, playing my Electrical Storm card, hoping to pre-empt her next strike.

We went on like that for hours. I was stronger in the seventeenth century, and she was stronger in the twenty-first. Just when one of us would get close to winning, the other one would play the Time Travel card and move the game to the era where she dominated.

At some point, I stopped being a spy and started being a teen having a good time. By nightfall, we had been playing for more than four hours, and still no one had won.

"Is this game going to go on forever?" I asked.

"I think it's a loop," she said. "We seem to have evenly matched decks."

"What does that mean?" I asked.

She grinned. "It means we should enter tomorrow's tournament as a team," she said. "Pairs divide up in different ways. Sometimes one player does offense and the other does defense. Sometimes one has a deck that features one of the superheroes more prominently. A past/present division of labor could be great for us."

"Can we see each other's hands during the game?" I asked.

She looked shocked. "Absolutely not," she said. "Partners sit across from each other and can't look at what the other person has."

"But we know each other's decks," I said.

"Yes, but part of the tournament game is that everybody buys a ten-card booster pack and opens it at the table," Imani said. "You pick ninety cards, and then you get whatever's in your additional ten-card deck. That way, even your partner doesn't know exactly what you have."

"Ah," I said. "Pretty smart."

"And lucrative," Imani said. "Guaranteed sales of four packs per table, plus the hourly drink minimum. These cafés clean up during tournaments."

"They do Magic: The Gathering on Friday nights," I said. "We nearly got kicked out last night when it started up."

Imani shook her head. "Those kids are hard-core," she said.

We walked over to the clipboard at the front of the café and signed up for the tournament. Then we each bought a couple packs of cards to strengthen our decks.

As we walked out onto the street, I assumed we would go back to my house to brush up for the tournament. But then I realized we were supposed to have just met.

"Wanna come over for dinner so we can prep for tomorrow?" I asked.

"I guess I can," she said with a shrug.

"Great," I said, and pretended to show her the way to my house.

My booster pack didn't have anything special. A couple so-so cards, one where you can initiate ten enslaved Africans at once, and another where you can strip the twenty-first-century villain of the superpower of your choice.

Imani got one fabulous card. "The Hurricane!"

"What does that do?" I asked.

"It takes you to the present and automatically restores the lives of any of your superhero trio who've been killed in the past."

"Fantastic," I said. "Whose deck should that go in?"

"Mine, I think," she said. "I'm playing the twenty-first century, so I'll know when I have the cards to really decimate them in present time."

"Okay," I said. "I'll also give you the modern villain power-stripper. Can you give me the spell to lift the blight on the sugarcane?"

We did some swapping, and eventually we each had a power deck—mine for the past and hers for the present.

We were ready for the tournament, and I was getting into the game so much that I almost forgot the assignment.

Almost, but not quite. When I said goodnight to Mom, she was still monitoring white supremacist websites.

The look on her face reminded me what was at stake in the mission. We had to take this terrorist down.

SEVENTEEN

On Sunday morning, the town was quiet, except for dressed-up families going to early church services. A pair of Latina girls in poufy dresses—one pink, one yellow—chased each other into a storefront with a big cross in the window.

But when I turned onto the street with the café, there were signs of life. It was only eight, but Imani had gotten there before me, and she wasn't the first one in line. A dozen other teens, some in cosplay outfits, were already there. I saw two Arantxas and one BaguaNi.

"You ready for this?" I asked.

"Definitely."

Across the street, the donut shop was doing brisk business, and several of the kids waiting in the café line had crinkled white paper bags in their hands.

At 8:45, Ramón and Kyle—*Kyle* and Ramón— showed up and got in line.

When they spotted me, Kyle held their place while Ramón walked over to us.

"What do we have here?" Ramón asked.

"A power team," I said, and introduced Imani.

"I haven't seen you around," he said. "Do you go to Calvin Coolidge?"

"I'm homeschooled," Imani said.

"Where'd you learn to play Triángulo?" he asked.

"I played once or twice at Game-Along Café in Mesa," Imani said. "I used to play with my cousin, but he went off to college."

"Partner play is really different from a two-person game," Ramón said.

"I know," Imani said. "My cousin had friends. The two of us beat a lot of them."

"Okay," Ramón said. "I know a challenge when I hear one. Good luck."

The tournament master, wearing a hooded black velvet cloak, started calling out people's names. Kyle and Ramón were paired against two Asian kids who looked like middle-schoolers. Imani and I waited anxiously for our names to be called.

Imani looked down at the San Diego ComxCon poster. "How come the female superheroes have waists so tiny that they couldn't really have any internal organs?"

"Right?" I said. "Like one of their superpowers is digesting food without a stomach or intestines."

"Yeah," Imani said. "She's got the chest room for lungs, but no room for a kidney or liver or, like, a spleen. Not that I know what a spleen does."

"How do these women ever have kids?" I asked. "There might be room in there for a uterus, but ovaries? No way. Fallopian tubes? Forget it."

"You don't usually see female superheroes eat," Imani said. "I guess you don't see them pregnant, either."

"The kids must just spring out of their heads," I said. "Like Athena sprang from Zeus."

"That's a possibility," Imani said. "But I think these women are definitely hiding something in their cleavage."

"A baby?" I asked.

"It's either there or in their butt," Imani said.

"You know that's not how the female reproductive system works, right?" I asked.

"Nothing else on this woman is anatomically correct," Imani said. "Why should that part be?"

"Imani Kennedy and ANN-drea Burke," the tournament master called.

We stood up, and he ushered us to a table with a

pair of white guys who looked like they might be in college.

After everyone was seated, the tournament master handed out booster packs, and we opened ours. The four of us fanned out our cards in our hands, hidden from everyone else.

"Yes!" I said when I saw that my pack included two cards for time travel and a Hurricane Changes Course card. You can play those on your world or your opponent's.

"No talking across the table," one of the guys said.

"What?" I asked. "I just said 'yes.'"

"She's new," Imani told them. She turned to me: "Just a brushup on the rules, ANN-drea. You're not allowed to address your partner directly. Which you didn't. However, if you have that kind of spontaneous talking five times in a game, the other team can submit a grievance. You never know if players have developed a code."

"Got it," I said. The other team looked appeased.

We rolled the dice to see who would go first. I rolled a two. Imani a five. One of the guys on the other team rolled a six, so they started.

It was so much more nerve-racking to play in a pair. I didn't know what Imani had, only that we had made her deck stronger in present time. I certainly didn't know what the strengths and weaknesses of the other team were.

We eventually got into a rhythm. It became clear what the other team was doing. One of them was playing offense, and the other was playing defense. I played right before the offense guy, so I created problems he had to address on his turn, and got both of them playing defensively. Once we had them in trouble, I played a card to get us into the present, and Imani began, systematically, to take them down.

I had dealt a major blow to their superheroes, and their villain had full power. The guy playing had to choose between making an offensive or a defensive move. He chose defense and restored power to one of his heroes. But Imani was too close to winning, and with a Synergy card, she put together all our present-time superheroes. At that moment in the game, we had enough power to completely destroy the present-time villain and freeze us in time for a whole round.

That left the other guy on their team with only one shot to keep them in the game. He would need to do something in offense that would be strong enough to put us back in jeopardy. And it would have to be in the present. But he was the defensive player, and he didn't have the cards. His mouth contracted into a tight lipless line.

"That's the game," he said.

My mouth opened. "Really?" I asked.

"Yes!" Imani said.

"Dude," said the guy who had conceded. "I told you, keep up the offense."

"Did you get that card in the booster deck?" the other guy asked Imani.

"The Synergy card?" she asked. "No way, it's one of my best."

"Can I see the rest of your deck?" he asked.

"Sorry," Imani said. "We may face off again at some point. I can't give anything away."

The two guys stood up and began arguing about whether or not an offensive player should play defense when they were in trouble.

"Great strategy," I said to Imani.

We debriefed and decided we'd try the same strategy for the rest of the day, with a few modifications. Players talked. It was possible that these two guys would gossip to others about our strategy. We made sure we each had a couple of strong cards in the era that the other was leading in. That way, even if the next team knew our strategy, we'd each have a secret weapon.

I shouldn't have been surprised when Ramón and Kyle—Kyle and Ramón—were our opponents in the second round. Half the competition had been taken out. There were only about a dozen tables in the place, and a bunch had already moved to round two.

"Grasshopper?" Ramón said.

Kyle laughed. "I take it Ramón has been teaching you," he said.

"He used to teach me," I said. "Until I met Imani." I introduced her to Kyle. We all shook hands and sat down.

"You beat the UA guys?" Ramón asked.

"The who?" I asked.

"University of Arizona," Imani said. Like she was from there. She was so good.

"Oh, yeah," I said. "We beat them. Easy peasy." It hadn't been that easy, but it was always good to psych out your opponent.

"Did they split it offense-defense?" Ramón asked.

I opened my mouth to speak, but Imani put a finger over her lips. "Some people," she said, tearing open her booster pack, "like to get info from the team challenging them in the form of chitchat."

I smiled at Ramón. "I don't really know what their strategy was," I said, "since I'm so new at this. Kind of like I just fell off a turnip truck from Los Angeles."

Ramón smiled. "I see your new teacher has some potential," he said as he opened his pack.

We were all quiet for a while, adding our booster cards to our decks. In the second round, you had to make a new deck with 110 of your best cards before you opened the second booster pack. Then you had to whittle down that new 120-card deck to 100.

I got a bunch of good cards in the present. Nothing spectacular from the seventeenth century, but some good old standbys. Imani said it was better to have your strongest cards than to focus on the era. I put together my deck and waited for the round to start.

We rolled the dice, and this time Imani went first. She opened with a bold move, setting the game in the past and blighting their sugarcane.

I grinned. She was purposefully throwing them off. Kyle played a strong seventeenth-century card, and I played a medium one. I didn't want to seem like that was my strongest era.

As near as I could tell, they fell for it. Imani kept playing strong in the past, and I played just below her. Then Ramón changed to the present, and we both began to play all out. She continued to outplay me, but by then, it just looked like she was the stronger player. We moved back and forth between eras and kept chipping away at them.

Two hours later, I still had all my strongest cards for the seventeenth century when Imani played a Time Travel card and sent us back to the past. This was the signal for me to go for the win.

I met her eyes. She didn't show anything, but I could tell what she had in mind.

In four rounds, I blighted their sugarcane, sent a military ship from Spain after their Maroon colony, and froze us in the past for two rounds. Imani didn't have much strong stuff left to play, but I had all my best cards. I got all our enslaved Africans freed and, above all, played the Lightning Strike card on our young enslaver, so he could never learn the secret of the Triángulo, and he couldn't ever become a villain in the present.

Ramón's and Kyle's mouths fell open.

"You had the Bewitching card the whole time?" Ramón asked.

"We can debrief after we win," Imani said. "Unless you have a card to undo the spell."

Ramón had played three Spell Reversal cards in the early rounds of the game. You couldn't have more than four of the same card. Maybe he had another, but it was a long shot. There were a few cards that could undo a spell like this, but they were all very rare. He had played one earlier in the game that weakened us considerably, but we had fought our way back up.

"Carajo," he said, and slapped down his cards. "That's the game."

I was dying to debrief the game with Ramón: *I was scared you had another Time Travel card! Did you see I used that move you taught me?* But we were whisked right into a third-round game.

This time it was a boy-girl team. Ramón whispered to me they were seniors at a nearby high school. Originally from Venezuela, they had been playing for a decade. Not that I felt totally psyched out or anything.

I opened my booster pack and got nothing good I could use. There were a couple of medium cards, but I already had at least four of each. I hoped Imani had gotten something good.

Well, apparently not, because the game lasted less than an hour. These Venezuelans had all the killer cards, including the rare ones that must cost a ton of money online—that is, *if* you could even find them. They each had Hurricanes and, more than that, they had a Time-Suspension Spell card that allowed only them to deal blows to or from either era for the next two turns. They crushed us.

The next thing I knew, they were shaking our hands. "Bien hecho," the girl said to me. "Good game."

Dazed, I took her hand. I almost replied in Spanish before I caught myself. "Good game."

"Well done, Grasshopper," Ramón said to me. "To be flattened by the Venezuelans is to be flattened with honor."

"I do believe that's the shortest game I've ever played," Imani said.

"I guess I don't feel so bad now, knowing we would have had to face them if we'd won," Kyle said.

"We should compare decks," Ramón suggested.

"I can't wait to show you some of the cards I picked up in the booster packs today," I said, taking the rubber band off my pack.

"Not here," Ramón hissed. "You don't want the competition to see what you have."

"Aren't you guys the competition?" I asked.

"No way," Kyle said. "We're your buddies who have a newfound respect for you and great admiration for your new friend."

"We want to play in tandem with you if we ever go to a tournament with superteams," Ramón said.

"Okay," I said. "Let's go somewhere we can compare decks without prying eyes. The pizza place?"

Ramón shook his head. "We gotta go to work tonight," he said.

"Besides," Kyle said. "I wouldn't trust anyplace public."

"How about you two come over tomorrow after school and we compare decks there?" Ramón asked.

"Sure," I said. "I got time."

"Same here," Imani said.

"It's a date," Ramón said. And the two of them headed out.

Imani and I walked out onto the street. A knot of kids from Calvin Coolidge were clustered in front of the donut shop.

"What's with Ramón talking about a date?" Imani asked.

"I'm sure he didn't mean anything by it," I said.

"He was looking straight at you," she said.

"Was he?"

She crossed her arms. "ANN-drea," she said. "You're not a teenager right now, you're a spy. You can't afford to act clueless. Ramón likes you."

I closed my eyes. "I know," I said. "I think he was trying to tell me the other night. I went in the house before he could finish his sentence."

"Good," she said. "Kyle is the assignment."

"I *know*," I said. "What should we do?"

"It's fine," she said. "We can use it to our advantage since they live together. If Ramón likes you, he'll keep inviting you over to their house. Between the two of us, we can tag-team search the house and find the intel we need."

"And if that doesn't work?" I asked.

"That's plan A," Imani said. "Plan B is that I'll run interference. Make sure you get more chances to talk to Kyle. The important thing is that we got invited to their house. Good work."

"It was a team effort," I said. "And I'm not gonna celebrate until we stop that terrorist."

EiGHTEEN

By now, I had gotten used to some of the rhythms of high school. Long periods of quiet when students were in class, punctuated by loud, raucous passing periods where students exploded out of classrooms and moved through the hallways in waves.

We had end-of-term testing in most of our classes, so I didn't get to talk to Kyle during class, and he didn't show up to lunch.

We were supposed to be going over to their house after school, but we didn't have one another's numbers, so I couldn't call or text. Of course, I *had* Kyle's phone number, as well as his address and Social Security number; I had pulled up his mother's credit card numbers and even his online shopping accounts. But somehow it had just been awkward to ask for his or

Ramón's phone number when the expectation was that we would just see each other in school. But actually, that was a good thing, since it would give me an excuse to put the next part of my plan in play.

I waited in front of the school after last period as masses of students walked past. There was a line of kids waiting to get into the convenience store. Mandy and the First-Class crew looked me up and down with attitude as they strolled by in their pastel outfits. I wanted to say, *I rescued my people from slavery, saved the modern-day world several times, and made it to the final round of a tournament this weekend! What did you do, besides shopping at the mall?* but I needed to look for Ramón and Kyle. Kyle and Ramón.

I saw Ramón first.

"Hey," Ramón said.

We exchanged greetings all around.

"Is your new friend coming?" Kyle asked.

"I'll text her," I said. "I should get your numbers. I realized I didn't have any way to get in touch if you didn't come out. Where were you at lunch?"

"All the fourth-period PE classes got held in the gym because someone vandalized the teacher's locker," Ramón said.

"Ramón knows who did it, but he wouldn't say," Kyle said.

"I didn't say I know," Ramón said. "I said I suspected."

"The teacher might have let us go," Kyle said.

"Somebody wrote that he's a homophobe, and he is," Ramón said. "I didn't want to snitch, especially when I wasn't sure."

"Give me your phone," I said to Kyle.

"Why?" he asked.

"So I can call my phone from yours, and we'll have each other's numbers," I said.

"Here's my phone," Ramón said. I took it and called myself. After I put in the LA area code, I went on auto-pilot for a second and almost put in my old number, but then I recalled the number I had memorized, my phone number for the operation. My phone rang, and I gave his back.

"Now yours," I said to Kyle. "Hand it over."

While I was entering my number, I stuck a tiny micro-drive into the charger slot of his phone. It would copy everything on his phone, but it would take a while. I would need to get it out later. My phone rang again, and I gave Kyle back his phone.

I looked at my phone. Two missed calls. And a text.

"Imani says she's at the pizza place," I said. "Do we want anything?"

"Yes, please," said Kyle.

We texted her our order and walked over to the pizza place together.

The pizza was ready when we got there. Everybody threw down a few bucks. We folded up our slices and headed out.

"Did you play all your best cards?" Kyle asked. "Or were you holding out on us?"

"I don't know about this line of questioning," Imani said. "How do we know you're not trying to suss out all our secret weapons?"

"We want to develop a superteam," Ramón said. "For a big tournament. Like the ones they have at ComxCon in San Diego."

"Those happen only once a year," Imani said. "Most of the time, you'll be here, playing with us."

"We're trying to get you to think big," Ramón said. "To think beyond this little town."

"Sounds good to me," I said. "I'd like to get out of this little town and go to San Diego."

We ate our slices as we walked. Going on foot from the pizza place to their house helped me understand more of the town's geography.

We walked past a neighborhood that had mostly apartment buildings, along with several bars, a few mechanics, and a big place that sold tires.

"This is our home base," Kyle said.

"Yeah," I said, looking at the yellow stucco cottage. "I ran into your moms when I was exploring over the weekend."

"You both live here?" Imani said. "Are you related?"

"We've both got single moms," Ramón said. "They teamed up to rent a house."

"Cool," Imani said, and followed them up the porch stairs.

The living room had good light that streamed in from a wide pair of front windows. It illuminated a large plaid couch with a pile of clothes on it.

"Kyle, I can't believe you left this mess of laundry," Ramón said.

"It's clean," Kyle said. "I just didn't fold it."

Kyle disappeared up the stairs. Ramón swooped up a laundry basket and dumped the clean clothes into it.

"Here," Ramón said to the two of us. "Have a seat." He took the laundry and followed Kyle upstairs.

The house was warm and lived-in, the opposite of the place where my mom and I were staying. Other than the laundry, the place was neat. On the mantle behind the couch were photos of both families and some of the boys' artwork from when they were little.

I got up to check out the photos to see if there were any of Kyle's dad. There weren't, but in one small black-and-white picture, there seemed to be a hand around his mom's shoulder. Or maybe it was a leaf. I hoped that John Summer was just hidden by the frame.

I slipped that photo into my pocket when Kyle and Ramón were out of the room.

By the time we sat down, Kyle had reappeared with several boxes of Triángulo cards. Ramón was coming back down the stairs.

"Show-and-tell," Imani said, and pulled out several decks of her own.

"Makes my little deck and a half look pathetic," I said.

"Not pathetic," Imani said, patting my arm. "Just novice."

"Ouch," I said.

Ramón disappeared into the kitchen, and I could visualize his sunporch bedroom. I recalled the pile of Triángulo cards on the bookshelf.

We began to fan out our cards on the coffee table.

Ramón came back with five boxes of cards.

"Is that all you have?" I asked.

"Not at all," Ramón said. "These are just the good ones."

"Okay," Imani said. "Most sought-after card. What would it be?"

"The Trance," said Kyle. "That card puts all the opponent's superheroes into a stupor for two turns."

"No way," said Ramón. "The Initiation." He explained that this card was stellar if you also had the New Moon Runaway card, which he did have. You could free everyone from slavery in two turns. Otherwise, you had to initiate each captive one by one, and they had to escape individually as well.

Imani laughed. "Someone kicked my butt with that last year."

"You've seen both of those cards in person?" Ramón asked.

"No," Imani said. "Only the New Moon card."

"They have counterfeit Initiation cards in Tijuana," Ramón said. "But they can't replace the hologram."

I was only half listening to the conversation. From the moment I came into the house, I had been keeping an eye on Kyle's phone. I needed to get my hands on it again to remove the copying device.

"Oh no," I said. "My phone died." I turned to Kyle. "Can I borrow yours to text my mom?"

"Sure," Kyle said, picking it up. "And you can borrow my charger, if you want. I should charge mine, too, but I have a double charger."

I could feel the tension in my chest. "Wait," I said. "Let's take a selfie first!"

"What?" Kyle asked. "Why?"

"We're a crew now," Imani chimed in. "We need a picture."

Imani grabbed his phone and handed it to me.

"I hate seeing myself in pictures," Kyle said.

"Then just pull your hood down to shade your face," Ramón said.

"Yeah," I said. "When we kick butt at some future tournament, we want to have a picture of the day it all began."

Imani stood in the center with me and Ramón on either side of her. Kyle lurked behind Ramón's shoulder, while I pretended to fidget with the camera a few times. I finally got the bug out.

I took a few shots. "This one is really good," I said.

"That's not a flattering angle," Imani said. "Let me take one. I got those long selfie arms."

We rearranged ourselves with her on the end. She took a few shots and, admittedly, they did look better. This time Ramón was in the middle. He put an arm around my waist. My skin tingled where his hand pressed against the fabric of my T-shirt.

"Now, that's a great picture," Imani said.

"Except for the fugitive-from-justice look Kyle's got going," Ramón said. "Otherwise, it's great."

After I texted my mom—just a note "updating" her about where I was—and gave the phone back, Kyle took his hood off and plugged his phone in, then offered me the charger. I had to turn my phone facedown, or it would be a dead giveaway that I had plenty of battery life.

For the next hour, we compared cards. I didn't really know enough to understand which cards were the most exciting, but Imani did. I just tried to *oooh* and *aahhh* along with the group.

I asked to use the bathroom, but unfortunately, Kyle took that moment to go in the kitchen and grab some chips. The half bath was off the kitchen, so I didn't have much opportunity to snoop where I assumed Kyle's bedroom was.

I pulled the photo out of my pocket and opened the back of the frame. I had a vision of using my pocket knife to slice off a photo of John Summer. But apparently, Kyle's mom had beat me to it. There was just a cropped-off shoulder in a plaid shirt. I put the photo in my pocket, flushed the toilet, washed my hands, and came back out.

As I returned to the living room, I waited till Kyle and Ramón were hunched over some cards on the coffee table and put the photo back on the mantle behind the couch.

All I'd learned was that John Summer liked plaid and whoever bought hand soap for the household liked lavender.

When we got home, Mom asked, "Did you get it?"

"Yeah," I said. "The little bug almost got stuck."

"I know," she said. "I hate those."

"She did great with it," Imani said. "I thought I might have to help out, but she was a pro."

"Are you kidding me?" I asked. "I was so nervous. You think so well on your feet. I couldn't have done it without you."

We smiled at each other as Mom plugged the tiny disk into a drive, and we scanned the content. We searched "dad" and "father." We searched for "John" and "Summer." We couldn't find any sign of him.

"I'll do a more thorough review," Mom said.

"We'll have to search the house," Imani said. "Maybe I could go by while the rest of you are at school."

I shook my head. "Ramón's mom works from home during the day."

"Then our after-school hangout time is probably our best shot," Imani said.

"We need a rare Triángulo card," I said. "Something so amazing that they'll lose track of time for a little while."

"Brilliant!" Imani said. "Let's see what Jerrold can get for us."

"Do we say we got it in a booster pack?" I asked.

"No," Imani said. "Tomorrow, I'll tell them I was holding out on them. But I realized how cool they were, and I'm going to let them in on my *secret* secret weapon."

"The Initiation?" I asked.

"If Jerrold can get it," she said.

By bedtime, Mom still hadn't found any sign of John Summer in Kyle's drive. And Jerrold had sent a text saying, "I'll see what I can do."

NINETEEN

Before lunch the next day, Imani sent a text saying "got it." I sent a group text that we'd all meet after school at the guys' house and that Imani had something to show us.

"Did she say what it was?" Kyle asked on the walk home.

"Nope," I said. "Just that we passed some kind of test. Now she's seen we're cool, she decided to show us her *secret* secret weapon."

"I wonder what it could be," Ramón said.

"All I know," I said, "is that it's a good thing we took that selfie. She sees us as her crew now."

"I guess so," Kyle said.

When we got to the house, Imani was already sitting on the plaid couch.

"I gave your guest a soda," Ramón's mom, Alma, said. "When you have company, you should offer them something to drink."

"We had popcorn yesterday," Ramón said.

"And water," Kyle said.

"You kids have fun," Alma said.

I watched her disappear into the study alcove in the kitchen.

"May I use your bathroom?" Imani asked.

That was my cue.

"I'm next," I said.

"There's another one," Ramón said. "Just go to the left at the top of the stairs."

"Thanks," I said.

At the top of the stairs, I closed the bathroom door and crept toward the bedrooms.

The first bedroom I opened was the master bedroom. There were two full-size beds on opposite sides of the room. The moms, I guessed.

In the next bedroom, there was a bunk bed; the lower bunk was covered in clothes. Yes. This must be Kyle's room.

Through the open door, I heard voices from downstairs. Imani must be back from the bathroom.

"Holy crap," I heard Kyle say. "How long have you had this?"

I crept deeper into the room. And success—the

laptop was sitting on the desk. I pulled out my tiny flash drive and put it into the USB port. It started copying everything automatically.

Like the phone copier, it didn't stick out. It wasn't noticeable, unless you actually looked into the port. But you had to pull it out with a fingernail, which was tricky.

I went back downstairs and, sure enough, the boys were drooling over Imani's Initiation card.

"I only played it once," Imani was saying. "My last game in Mesa. Once people know you have a card like this, it gets around town. They don't want to play against you, because you have such an advantage."

"Have I mentioned how much I love being on the same team with you?" Ramón said.

"We haven't even played together," Imani said.

"Not yet, but now that I know what you have," Ramón said, "I'll never play against you again."

The four of us played for the rest of the afternoon. The Initiation card stayed on the table, faceup, like a talisman.

Ramón and Kyle were good hosts, giving us lots of beverages, so I was able to take a second trip upstairs to the bathroom, and this time I actually needed to go. I washed my hands and got the drive out on my way back down.

The upstairs bathroom soap was lavender, too.

Later that evening, Mom and I sat at the blond wood kitchen table in our fake house and searched the data from the laptop.

"Let's start with the low-hanging fruit," Mom said. "The Factory was able to hack both of Kyle's free email accounts. But the school account was much harder. We're hoping he saved the password on this computer."

She handed me our laptop, now loaded with all the data from Kyle's computer, and had me pull up the school email portal. I hovered over the sign-in boxes and, sure enough, a username and password came up. I worried for a moment that it would be Ramón's, but it was Kyle's.

It only took us a quick search to find what we were looking for—an email from John Summer! It was from about a year ago.

> Dear Kyle,
> Hello, son. I've been wanting to write to you
> for a long time, but wasn't sure how I could
> contact you directly. Now that you're older, I
> google you from time to time. And this time
> I finally found something, a story in the local
> paper about a cleanup day at your school.
> There you were in the back row of the photo!
> Almost the tallest in the class. I couldn't
> believe you're taller than the teacher. But of

course you are. Your mother and I are both pretty tall.

I know she doesn't want to hear from me after all this time. You need to know that what happened between her and me had nothing to do with how I feel about you. I think about you every day. I couldn't help but take a stab at figuring out your school email address. I hope I got it right. Maybe some other KyleSummer@students.CarsonAZ.net is getting this email. There's so much I want to tell you about everything that's happened since I left Arizona. But first I want to hear about you. So handsome. I bet the young ladies are quite taken with you. Is there anyone special? But I'm getting ahead of myself. First of all, happy birthday! I can't believe you're thirteen. I hope to hear back from you soon.
With love,
your dad
John

I clicked on the sender's profile, but it was just that shadowy silhouette of a man's head. I usually thought that meant an email user was lazy, but with John Summer, I was sure it was intentional. I looked in

Kyle's folders and found several outgoing emails from Kyle to his dad, but they were all drafts. All unsent.

From KyleSummer@students.CarsonAZ.net:

Dad,

From KyleSummer@students.CarsonAZ.net:

John,

From KyleSummer@students.CarsonAZ.net:

Hey.

Mom got on the phone with Jerrold immediately, and they began tracking the email address. It wasn't one of the ones that the terrorist had used to post on message boards previously.

A half an hour later, we got a call back.

"Great work," Jerrold said. "We tracked this back to a public library computer in rural Oregon. He hasn't logged into this account for a couple of months. Looks like he checked every day after he sent Kyle that email. Then it slowly scaled back to a few times a week, then weekly, then once a month, then nothing."

"I guess he realized the kid wasn't gonna write back," Mom said.

"But now that we have Kyle's password, we can hack the account," Jerrold said. "We'll send an email to John Summer that will look like it's from Kyle but will redirect to us."

"But that will only work if John Summer checks this account," Mom said.

"We're using every lead we possibly have to catch this guy," Jerrold said. "And this is still good. It pinpoints Summer's location at a particular time. Trust me, every data point matters, and we'll get an agent up to Oregon to see if he can track him down. But keep digging. See what else you can find."

The laptop data took much longer to sort through than the phone. Once again, we tried "dad" and "father," but there were too many hits. We also tried "John" and "Summer" but were inundated by the random ways that they came up.

"Can you do a case-sensitive search?" I asked Mom.

"I do that first," she said. "But sometimes people don't capitalize, and we don't want to miss anything."

The two of us began the arduous process of investigating every hit on the search terms.

Kyle and his mother both had the last name Summer, so even when it was case-sensitive, there was no way to narrow it to search exclusively for Kyle's dad. Also,

Kyle had gone to John F. Kennedy Middle School, so "John" came up countless times as well. All our search terms were so common, they came up over and over in irrelevant emails. And they also came up in irrelevant documents on the computer. Like the paper Kyle wrote on "My Summer Vacation." Or several mentions of "Father McKenzie" in Beatles lyrics that somebody had downloaded.

After two hours searching through emails and term papers and calendar entries and downloaded PDFs, I was getting frustrated. "John Summer" didn't have any hits, but if we were going to search through every single "Summer," it was going to be a long night.

"What's the dad's middle initial?" I asked.

"L," Mom said.

"For what?" I asked.

"Leopold."

I searched for it and, unexpectedly, it came up.

"I've got something," I said to my mom as I pulled up the result.

A chat exchange.

Heather.mcclelland: I didn't know John had a kid.

Kyle353: Easy to miss. Hasn't been around since I was really little.

Heather.mcclelland: Are we sure it's the same guy? There

are a lot of guys named John with the last name
Summer. It would be a weird coincidence, but it's
definitely possible.

Kyle353: Not with the middle name Leopold.

Heather.mcclelland: His middle initial is L. But I don't
know what it stands for.

Kyle353: Trust me. It's Leopold. How long have you
known him?

Heather.mcclelland: We've been dating on and off for a
few years.

We had another line on John Summer! But who the
heck was Heather McClelland?

I scrolled back to read the rest of the exchange, and
we learned that Heather McClelland was a woman that
Kyle had contacted on Craigslist to buy a few decks
of Triángulo cards. They had an awkward interaction
about John, and then Kyle declined to buy the deck.

That was a few months ago. The team immediately
began searching for everything they could find on
Heather McClelland. It was the best lead we had so far.

On her social media, they didn't find any photos
of John Summer, but they did find some posts about
her dating a "mysterious new guy from out of town."

These were from several years before. She changed her status back and forth between "in a relationship" and "single" for a while. She had been "single" for the last six months. But that didn't mean they weren't still in contact.

"Now what?" I asked.

"They might get someone to question her," said Mom.

"What if we could get her to turn up at Kyle's house?"

"Are you going to work a few miracles?" Mom asked.

"No," I said, opening up a Craigslist window and running a quick search. "We have her username. It looks like she sells a lot of different stuff. If she's selling more Triángulo cards, I may be able to set a meetup at Kyle's."

"That's a great idea," Mom said. "Let's see if we can make it happen."

TWENTY

The rest of the week was spent mostly just pretending to be a student. I had no idea that regular school had this much homework!

After the final bell on Friday, I waited for Kyle and Ramón in front of school as the students poured out of the building. Calvin Coolidge was pretty evenly divided between mostly white and Latine students. Imani would have been easy to pick out of the crowd, being both Black and tall. Kyle was pale and tall, but he walked with a slouch, making him hard to spot. I tried looking for Ramón, who had better posture. This turned out to be a mistake, because Kyle came out alone and I almost missed him.

"Where's Ramón?" I asked.

"He picked up a shift at work," Kyle said. "Is Imani coming?"

"Yeah," I said. "She texted me that she'd be there."

As the two of us walked toward his house, it occurred to me that this was my time alone with Kyle. Maybe I'd be able to quiz him about his dad.

We made small talk on the way: tests, papers due. His phone buzzed, and when he answered it, I sent Imani a quick message. "Don't come. Text in fifteen minutes you can't make it."

When we got to his house, my phone sounded a message.

"Dang," I said. "Imani can't make it. I should've known. This day is the worst."

Kyle asked tentatively, "What's wrong?"

"They did an annoying Father's Day thing in art," I said. "Like I could just make some kind of card and send it to a ghost."

"Your dad's dead?" he asked.

"He left when I was a baby," I said. "I don't remember him. I just remember my mom being really sad when I was little." I was improvising. "There are three bad days in the year: the anniversary of the day he left, when my mom gets depressed; his birthday; and Father's Day, which always gets me." My cover was supposed to be that my parents were getting divorced. But the guy in LA who dumped my mom could be a stepdad. It could have been a second marriage. My team and I would clean up the story behind the scenes. I had told the original cover story to Ramón, but this was better. I was opening up to Kyle more, making it so that we had a similar situation.

"I know what you mean," Kyle said. "My dad's been gone most of my life."

"It's, like, this sort of invisible thing," I said. "Because nobody expects your dad to be the one to pick you up from school anyway, or to come to the birthday party. Nobody has to know unless you tell them. And then it's this awkward heavy moment. I don't know your exact story, but somehow I knew you'd understand."

"I wonder if things would be different if my dad was around . . . If they would have turned out . . . differently."

"If what would've turned out differently?" I asked.

"Just . . . like, being in a family can affect a guy. The way he turns out. Like sort of . . . I don't know . . . determine what type of man he turns out to be."

Was this it? Was this where Kyle was going to tell me about how he thought his dad might not have gone off the rails and become a white supremacist if only his parents had stayed together?

I nodded and waited for him to continue.

"It's probably stupid," Kyle said. "Just something that people say."

"It doesn't sound stupid to me," I said.

"I just . . . I wonder because . . . I'm gay. And not having a dad . . . I feel like people might . . . you know, psychoanalyze that."

He was gay? Kyle was gay? I'd totally missed that!

"You're probably the first person I've told outside our family," he said. "I hope that's not too weird. Ramón knows. Our moms, too."

"I'm really honored that you would . . . you know, tell me," I said. "People are who they are. And they love who they love. It's not about . . . like some problem in their family made them gay or anything."

"I guess . . ." Kyle said. "Thanks."

"Totally."

I had just assumed he was straight. I tried not to buy into stereotypes, but I guess subconsciously I expected gay guys to dress better or to be into pop divas instead of nerdy fantasy worlds.

"Do you think your dad would have been . . . homophobic?" I asked. "Was he, like, conservative?"

"He was kind of a back-to-nature guy," Kyle said. "Really off the grid."

"Like a survivalist?" I asked.

"Kind of," he said. "He liked to be out by himself in nature a lot. I don't know."

"Do you have any idea where he is?"

"No," he said. "We sent letters to a PO box, but then it closed."

"Here in town?"

"No," Kyle said. "Somewhere in Oregon."

I filed that away.

"He sent me an email last year," Kyle said. "But he

was like, 'The ladies must really like you,' and I was like . . . what could I even say to that? I never wrote back."

"Does your mom know?" I asked.

He shook his head. "She'd want to talk about it," he said. "I couldn't deal."

"It's so weird when people just disappear," I said. "Did your dad have any other ties here in town? Other family?"

"Nope," Kyle said.

"Was he even from around here?" I asked. I knew he'd been born in Ohio.

Kyle shook his head. "I think I've maxed out on the dad talk. Can we change the subject?"

"Sure," I said. "Does the school have a GSA or something we could go to?"

"GSA?"

"You know, gay/straight alliance club?" I asked.

Kyle looked stricken. "I'd never go to that," he said. "Maybe that's cool in LA but not here."

He had a point. I couldn't imagine being out as a gay teen at Calvin Coolidge High School.

"So . . ." he said. "You wanna play?"

It took me a moment to realize he meant Triángulo.

"Yeah," I said. "Let's do it."

We set out the cards, and he kicked my butt for an hour.

◆ ◆ ◆

It was a welcome break from losing when Ramón came in.

"Where's Imani?" he asked.

"Some homeschool appointment thing," I said.

"How's the game?" Ramón asked.

"Kyle is crushing my uprising," I said. "I need a teammate."

"No fair," Kyle said.

"Okay, fine," I said. "I'll try to lose with dignity."

I lost with dignity, and then watched Kyle and Ramón play.

Kyle's mother came into the living room. The other times we had met were brief, but this time I could really check her out while Kyle and Ramón were focused on the Triángulo game. Emily Summer was tall and solidly built. Her blond hair was darker at the roots, pulled back in a loose ponytail at the nape of her neck. Did she know she had been married to a white supremacist? Was still legally married to him?

I went back to watching the game. Had John Summer shared any of those ideas with Emily when they were together? Or did he get radicalized after he left this family? She couldn't really share his ideas if she had built a life with a Latine family, could she?

Emily turned to me and said they were having lasagna for dinner. She asked if I wanted to stay. I heartily agreed.

"I'm supposed to meet someone around five

forty-five," I said. "But she's just dropping something off. Is it okay if I ask her to come by here?"

"Of course."

I texted Kyle's address to Heather McClelland. I felt guilty. I believed Kyle had no idea where his dad was. His mom seemed nice and didn't deserve to have her night ruined. But lives might be at stake, and I couldn't let hurt feelings stand in the way of my job.

The lasagna was almost ready. An amazing smell of bubbling tomato sauce and melted cheese was wafting in from the kitchen when the doorbell rang.

"I'll get it, Mamá," Ramón said.

Mamá. Just hearing Spanish made me homesick for my family. The rest of my family. The rest of myself.

"It's probably for me," I said, following him to the door.

The woman on the porch was blond and in her thirties.

I looked over Ramón's shoulder. "Ms. McClelland," I said. "Thanks for coming, and for rolling with the change of plans."

"No problem," she said.

"Come on in," Ramón said.

"Ms. McClelland is selling me a super booster pack of Triángulo cards," I said as she came in.

"Please call me Heather," she said.

"Okay, Heather," I said. "These are my friends, Kyle

Summer and Ramón Santiago. They taught me how to play Triángulo." I watched her face as I deliberately said Kyle's last name.

Heather stared at Kyle. "Kyle Summer? Didn't you contact me about Triángulo cards a while back?"

He looked startled.

"You know each other?" Ramón asked.

"We just emailed," Kyle mumbled. "I never bought anything."

"I'm really sorry, ANN-drea," Heather said. "I think I should head out."

"You haven't sold me the deck yet," I said.

"Here," Heather said. "Take it. Don't worry about the money. I should go."

"Did I miss something?" I asked. "Why is this weird all of a sudden? Is it illegal to sell Triángulo cards?"

"Nothing like that," Heather said. "It's just—I have this sort of on-again, off-again thing with Kyle's dad."

"Who is it?" Emily asked, walking through the swinging kitchen door into the living room.

"Wait," I said. "You dated Kyle's dad?" I was going for befuddled, but I said it loudly and clearly.

Emily froze. "You what?" she asked, her face reddening and hardening. "Who are you?"

"Oh my God," I said. "I didn't realize—I was just buying Triángulo cards from, um, Heather, off the internet."

"And you come in here telling me you're dating John?" Emily twisted the dish towel in her hands.

"I'm so sorry," I said. "I shouldn't have—"

"No, honey," Emily said to me. "You haven't done anything wrong. Heather, please get out and please tell my husband to send the darn child support."

"Husband?" Heather said. "You're still *married*?"

"He left thirteen years ago," Emily said. "Never bothered with any divorce papers."

"Look," Heather said. "I'm sorry. I had no idea. I'm getting to the bottom of this. I'm sorry to have interrupted your evening." She rushed out.

"I . . . thanks for the dinner invitation," I said. "I should go, too." I picked up my jacket. "See you at school."

As I went out the front door, Ramón came after me. "Let me walk you home," he said.

"Uh . . . okay . . . sure," I said.

We walked down Washington Street. "Oh God, I feel so bad," I said.

"You had no way of knowing that woman dated Kyle's dad," Ramón said.

"I . . . guess," I said. "She said dat*ing*. Off and on. Like they're still together."

"Yeah, but still," he said. "Not your fault."

A loud motorcycle zoomed by, vibrating the pavement.

"Thanks for walking me," I said. "I feel terrible. I

was just getting to know Kyle better. He even came out to me."

"That he was gay?" Ramón said.

"You'd better hope so," I said. "Otherwise, you'd be outing him."

"Sorry," Ramón said. "You're right. I'm just shaken up about the girlfriend."

"Yeah," I said. "I feel guilty I didn't pay her."

"Should we look at the deck?" Ramón asked.

"Sure," I said, pulling it out of my pocket.

As we continued through the warm evening toward my house, we flipped through the deck. Our pace slowed, and we found a couple half-decent cards, including the Middle Passage. Ramón explained that if your opponent had freed all the captives on their plantation, you could play this card to send a ship with a new crew of kidnapped Africans to work.

"And they have to start all over to free them?" I asked.

"Yep," he said.

"That's brutal," I said.

"Slavery was a brutal institution," he said.

I nodded, and we walked in silence for a few blocks.

A car drove by playing a pop song with a heavily auto-tuned female voice. "Hey, boys! Hey, hey, boys!" she sang. She had that fake sexy whine in her voice that made me cringe inside.

We didn't speak until we were in front of my house.

"I just—" I began. "Do you think it's gonna be okay

for Kyle and his mom? I look back and see I said all the wrong things."

"Kyle's mom is tough. She blows up, but she's fine by the next day. I've seen her way more upset than that."

"You really think so?" I asked.

"I don't just think so," Ramón said. "I know."

"Okay," I said. "I should go."

"Wait," Ramón said. "I need to tell you something."

"What?" I asked. He had that look again. Before Kyle came out to me, I had a really clear reason to go inside before Ramón could say anything, but now that I knew there was no chance Kyle was interested in me in that way, I probably should still go . . . shouldn't I? Yes, I definitely should. But the weakening in my resolve delayed me. Before I could formulate an excuse, he was talking again.

"ANN-drea, I like you," he said.

"I like you, too," I said cautiously.

"No," he said. "I *like* you . . . like . . . have feelings for you."

"Oh," I said. I swallowed. "I like you, too." I looked down at the pavement. I couldn't quite face him when I said it. "That same way."

"You're so—" he said. "So not what I expected. I mean, on day one you were sitting with the First-Class girls, but you're nothing like them. It's like the way you look and your personality are so different . . . What is it about you?"

"I don't know," I said.

He was leaning forward, like he was going to kiss me. Time slowed down. He was inching closer, and my heart was beating like crazy. He was inches from my face.

"Ramón!"

Ramón jumped back. Not just like he was startled. He jumped all the way back.

The kid was maybe half a block away. A Latino kid on a bike.

And the way Ramón looked when his eyes flitted from the guy to me, then down to the pavement. He looked . . . almost . . . ashamed.

What was I doing? I was a spy. I couldn't kiss someone in the operation. Especially not someone who seemed . . . embarrassed to be seen with me.

"I gotta go," I said, and ran up the stairs.

Ramón stood frozen in place.

Through the slit in the curtains, I watched the young Latino roll up to him. He looked familiar. I'd probably seen him at school. They gave some kind of handshake hug and walked away together, the kid wheeling the bike beside him. I tried to convince myself I was spying on him as part of the assignment, but I knew this was the surveillance of a girl who was almost but not quite kissed.

TWENTY-ONE

Mom wasn't home. I sat down on the couch feeling rattled. I looked at the animals in the curio cabinet. They were big-eyed in shock, staring questions at me. *Did that really just happen? What are you going to do now?*

I needed to check in with someone from my team. I texted Imani and asked her to come over. She was nearby and able to get to me in five minutes. Which was good, because I was freaking out.

"I almost kissed Ramón," I blurted out. "We said we liked each other. We would have kissed except—we got interrupted . . ." I couldn't bring myself to explain what had happened and that look of shame on Ramón's face.

"It's gonna be okay," Imani said. "Don't panic."

"This is so unprofessional," I said. "From the

beginning, I've always been taught that you have to stay detached. It's why they never deploy kids younger than us. They're not mature enough to compartmentalize."

"It's not just about age," Imani said. "It's a skill. It takes time for any spy to learn. Whatever their age."

"It's not as bad as it sounds," I said, suddenly desperate to reassure her I had some professionalism left. "Kyle came out to me as gay. I didn't sabotage the primary assignment."

Imani blinked. "Did not see that coming," she said. "But seriously, even if you did, it'd be okay."

"I can't believe this," I said. "Everybody believed in me. Mom. Jerrold. The Factory. Everybody. And I'm ruining it with some crush?"

"It's not ruined," Imani said. "But when we talked before, about how Ramón liked you, you should have mentioned that you liked him back. Then we could have strategized about how to respond if he said something."

"I know," I said. "I should have said something earlier. To Mom. At least to you. But I was sure I could just shut it down."

I had been pacing back and forth across the living room, but now I sank down into the couch. "I didn't want to be that girl. The one who screws up the assignment because of a crush. I feel so stupid."

"It's not you," Imani said, sitting down next to me. "It's . . . just the situation. Girls are taught that we're shallow and frivolous and boy crazy. We try so hard not to be that. But sometimes we meet someone we like, and we have feelings. We push them down. But the further down you push them, the more powerful they get."

"Don't I know it," I said.

"You're not alone," Imani said. "I've messed up the same way."

"Really?"

"Yes," she said. "But the real mistake I made was not to tell my team. You're not the first teen agent to have a crush. Dang, probably not the first adult agent, either."

"Why do I feel so embarrassed?" I asked.

"It's human nature," Imani said. "People get crushes. Sometimes the person likes you back. It's nothing to be ashamed of, whether you're a spy or not."

"So when you have a crush, you don't feel half mortified, half elated?" I asked.

"Of course I feel that way," Imani said. "But I tell myself that it's natural, that there's nothing to be ashamed about, and I don't keep it a secret. At least not anymore."

"You don't feel like shrinking into the floor?"

"I absolutely do," Imani said. "That's the place where your spy resolve comes in. Where you suck it up. You bravely declare that you have feelings that are distracting you, so that your team can help."

"Will you just shoot me, instead?" I asked.

"I have not been issued a firearm," Imani said. "And I don't believe in shooting colleagues."

"Darn your integrity," I said.

"Besides," Imani said. "I'm living proof that your crush can get found out and you can survive."

"What do I do?" I asked.

"You need to report in to Jerrold and tell the truth," she said.

"To *Jerrold*?" I said, feeling nauseous. It felt good to confess to Imani, and I had been working up my nerve to tell my mom. But Jerrold?

"You can do this," Imani said.

I walked over and fished my phone out of my sweat-shirt pocket.

"No, I can't," I said, setting the phone on the arm of the couch. "Is it too late to quit this assignment?"

"Yes . . . but you're not alone," she said. "I'll hold your hand if you need me to. I'll even say the words myself, with your permission."

"Really?" I said. "You'd do that for me?"

"Of course, girl," she said. "I got you. I'll even write a rap if you need me to:

> *Jerrold, my girl got something to tell you*
> *Every spy has a time when their feelings just*
>   *seep through*
> *Her cover isn't blown*
> *But it's time you known*
> *She got a crush on Ramón.*"

I laughed so hard I couldn't stand. I collapsed onto the couch and laughed until my sides ached. Imani cracked up, too. Every time we started to calm down, we both kept feeling aftershocks of giggles.

"Please," I said, when I could speak again. "Please do not rap that to Jerrold on the phone."

"How you gonna disrespect my lyrical skills?" Imani said. "I totally freestyled that. Right off the head."

"I certainly hope it was spontaneous," I said. "Otherwise, that would mean you've been monitoring my internal love life and composing rap songs about it."

"The organization doesn't have that technology yet, but we're working on it," Imani said.

"No artistic support will be needed," I said. "I think I can spit it out. 'I have a crush on Ramón.'"

"I could do an interpretive dance in the background," Imani said. She stretched and twirled.

I started to laugh again, and it gave me a stitch in my side. "Must keep practicing," I said. "'I have a crush on Ramón.'"

"I think the textbook term is 'have developed romantic feelings for,'" Imani said.

"Maybe I'll be the one to shoot you," I said.

"Fortunately, you haven't been issued a firearm, either."

"I can't say the feelings part," I said, cringing. "Maybe I can focus on the action. I almost kissed Ramón. The feeling was mutual. I learned that Kyle was gay."

"Good, you've got a script going," Imani said. "Now, let's just rip off the Band-Aid." Imani handed me my phone.

As always, Jerrold was sharp-eyed and attentive. I had only known him a year, and he had always been supportive and direct. But I had never shared anything like this with him. Not with any adult.

I gazed at him through the video screen. Same neat and close-cropped hair. Same three-piece suit, the vest making him look dapper and old-timey. Same deep and calm voice.

"I—um—there's been a sort of development," I began.

"Rip off the Band-Aid," Imani murmured in my ear.

I closed my eyes and blurted out, "I found out Kyle's gay and I almost kissed Ramón."

I was surprised to hear a deep-voiced chuckle. I opened my eyes to see Jerrold trying to play it off as a cough.

"Are you laughing?" Imani asked.

Jerrold cleared his throat and spoke in his usual calm tone. "I am so sorry, girls," he said. "I did let out a chuckle of relief. When I saw both of you on the screen—your worried faces—I feared something horrible had happened. That I'd have to go to your parents and tell them I'd miscalculated terribly. That this mission was much more dangerous than we'd known. Bárbara was certainly not going to be happy."

"No," I said. "She would not be."

"But an almost kiss?" he asked. "That is no problem at all. And that the subject came out to you? A testament to your spycraft."

Imani squeezed my hand. I was so relieved that Jerrold wasn't going to kick me off the assignment.

"Keep up the good work," he said. "Just stick close to the subject and his family. You too, Imani."

"We're on it," Imani said.

"I'll see you soon," he said. "Thanks to your work, we think we may be closing in. I'm headed to Arizona tonight."

As Imani signed off, I was kind of choked up and couldn't speak. I didn't really expect them to be so understanding.

"You okay?" Imani asked.

I just nodded. Right then, I got a text from Mom that she was out in the field for most of the night. She would have Chinese food delivered for dinner, and I should reach out to Imani or Jerrold to debrief. I just texted back "ok," like I hadn't been debriefing with both of them for nearly an hour altogether.

"Okay," Imani said, standing up. "I should probably go."

"Wait," I said, finding my voice. "Can you stay? Sleep over?"

She blinked. "Sure," she said. "I don't see why not."

I didn't really want to talk anymore, so we found a reality TV show to watch. The girls on the show were much more of a mess than me, and I felt better.

I guess we fell asleep in front of the TV because the next thing I knew, my phone was ringing. Not my regular tone, but the emergency ring. Imani's was ringing, too.

"Jerrold?" I answered, my voice a croak. I fumbled for the remote to turn off the TV. It was one in the morning.

"The two of you need to get across town ASAP," he said. "Use a rideshare. I'm sending details."

Fortunately, we'd both fallen asleep fully clothed. We grabbed jackets and requested a ride to a location unknown. I grabbed my skateboard.

As Imani tracked the progress of our rideshare driver, I opened the message.

It was an audio recording from earlier that evening, from a Las Vegas pay phone to Heather McClelland's cell.

> **Man's voice:** I got your text. It's not what you think.
>
> **Heather McClellan's voice:** Why should I believe you?
>
> **Man:** I'm coming to see you.
>
> **HM:** A wife? A wife and a kid?
>
> **Man:** I'm getting in my car right now.

They had dispatched Operative 5571 (my mom!) to do surveillance on Heather's house. Heather had gotten a text at 12:53 that he was outside. Yet there was no sign of anyone at Heather's house. They had a wrong address for her in a town that was a half hour away. They did a geolocation on the phone and realized their mistake. The entire surveillance crew was in the wrong location. The only other operatives they had in town were me and Imani.

TWENTY-TWO

The town of Carson was quiet in the wee hours of the morning, nearly silent. The houses were dark, and the streets were empty. I didn't see a single car and only heard a few in the distance.

The car dropped us off in front of an apartment building. It was three stories high, with garden apartments. The doors opened into the parking lot. The lighting wasn't great. I thought we would have to work hard to find the right apartment in the dark, but I stopped worrying about that the moment we opened the car door. John Summer was making lots of noise on the ground floor.

"Come on, Heather," he said, banging on one of the doors. "Let me in."

There was no sound from the apartment. The exterior light was off.

Imani and I ducked behind an SUV. We lay on the parking lot asphalt, heads together. We could see him clearly from beneath the vehicle.

Summer was tall. He had on a faded denim jacket and olive-green cargo pants. His sandy hair hung below a dark army cap, falling nearly to his shoulders.

He paced back and forth for a while, but we couldn't see his face very clearly. Then he stopped. He stood and faced the door, clenching and unclenching his fists several times. Then he drummed his fingers on his outer thighs, like he was psyching himself up for something.

"I just want to talk to you," he said. "And I'm not leaving until I do. If I have to wait outside all night long, I will, Heather. You know I will."

"Fine," Heather said. Her voice came from inside and was a little muffled. "You can talk to me through the door."

"This is all just a misunderstanding," he said.

"A misunderstanding?" she said. "Last time we were together . . . what? Six months ago? You were talking about wanting to start a family with me. You didn't think you should mention that you *already had one*?"

"Heather, I can explain," John said. "Just let me in and I can explain everything."

"This is why we're not together, John." Heather's voice came through the door more clearly now. "All the secrecy and the disappearances. You always come to visit me but never let me visit you. Apparently, you never went back to this wife and kid. Who knows if you have more? Maybe a family in Oregon and another in Nevada? I'm done."

"Honey," he said. "It's not what you think. I live on the road. I'm supposed to be making a delivery to Colorado right now, but I came all the way down here so I could explain the situation. And I'm not gonna yell all my personal business to you through a closed door. Who knows who could be listening? If you'd only open the door."

Imani elbowed me, and I elbowed back.

He had his back to us, and the low-watt parking lot light shone down on him. His face was in total shadow.

"This is what I'm talking about, John," she said. "The paranoia. It's almost two in the morning. Who could possibly be listening? People are sleeping."

"The government never sleeps," John said. "Their surveillance is twenty-four hours a day."

"*I'm* trying to sleep," Heather said. "And don't bother to give me the new phone number you've gotten since I texted you yesterday. Don't give me a burner phone to contact you with. Please. Just go away. I'm not opening the door."

"Just let me in, baby," he said. "Come on. I've got deliveries in Colorado and in Montana. I came a long way to see you."

"I don't care if you came from Beijing, China," she said. "You're not welcome here, and I have half a mind to call the police."

No! I thought. The threat of police would chase him away. *Let him in. Let him stay for a few hours.*

His body clenched up, like he was going to yell. And then he did that thing again, where he balled his fists a few times and then tapped his fingers on the outside of his thighs.

"Please, honey," he said in a voice that was clearly struggling to stay calm. "Don't say that. Just talk to me, okay?"

"This is only gonna end one of two ways, John," Heather said. "Either you go away, or I call the police. That's it. Those are the choices."

"I can't believe you won't give me a chance to explain," he said.

"Give you a chance to explain?" Heather asked, her voice rising in outrage. "Every time we were together, I asked you about yourself, your past, your previous relationships. And every time you said what? There's nothing to tell. That's the past. You had your chance to explain. Now, go away before I call the cops."

"But, Heather," he said. "I drove all the way from Las Vegas. I'm exhausted. I need to sleep or I won't be safe on the road."

"You can sleep in your car," she said. "My therapist says I need to work on setting limits with how I let people treat me. So I will. You don't get to come running over here and demanding to talk to me in the middle of the night. It's disrespectful, John. I'm not going to stand for being disrespected like this. It's over between us, John. Over. Don't call me. Don't email me. And definitely don't show up at my place unannounced. I've given you plenty of second chances. And I'm done."

What she said made sense. Ordinarily I would have been glad to see a woman standing up for herself. But I wasn't a therapist—I was a spy. And we needed him to stay. Even half an hour would be long enough for our squad to arrive.

"Honey," John said. "Please."

"No, John," Heather said. "That's the limit. I'm going to bed now."

"Heather," he said. "Come on!"

Dammit. Could we take a photo of him? I opened the camera on my phone, but what would I capture? The back of his head?

"Goodbye, John," she said, her voice retreating back into the apartment.

John turned away from the door. In the moment when his face was illuminated by the limited light, I did a burst of photos. He had a shorter beard than in the surveillance video Jerrold had shown me, but there was something about his stance—it was definitely him. He was much older than he looked in his driver's license photo. And while his young face on the license was not really smiling, now his face was scowling. His hateful look gave me chills, and I was glad that he couldn't see me.

John Summer gave up and walked back to his car, a compact silver hatchback.

Imani and I crept to the far end of the SUV for a better view. I tried to read the front license plate, but it was mud splattered. I think it started with 7. I couldn't have said what state it was from.

"Dang," Imani whispered. "If she could have just kept him talking for a little while longer."

"Maybe he will take a nap," I said. "Maybe our team can still catch him."

But that hope died when he started the engine.

We looked at each other. "Let's at least try to see the back license plate," I suggested.

"He's not gonna drive off slowly enough," Imani said.

I had an idea. "I'm gonna cut him off!" I said. "See if you can read the back plate."

"ANN-drea, wait!" Imani said.

But I had already jumped on my skateboard and was heading toward his car. As I kicked to get going, I pulled my hood low over my face.

He put the car in gear. As he drove forward, I swerved into the path of his headlights. He braked suddenly, and I jumped off my board and tumble-fell, the way I had been taught. I landed clear, and the board rolled off into the dark.

That jerk didn't even stop to see if I was hurt. He just drove around me and off into the night.

Imani came running over to me. "Are you okay?" she asked.

"Did you get the plate number?" I asked.

"Mud splattered," she said.

"The rest of the car wasn't," I said. "Must have been intentional."

"But are you okay?" she asked.

"Rule number one from the girls who taught me to skateboard," I said. "Know how to fall. I might have a few bruises, but I'm fine."

"That was pretty reckless," Imani said.

"I prefer to think of it as spontaneous," I said.

She laughed.

"We didn't get the plate or manage to stall him until our team got here," I said.

"What about the photos?" she asked.

"I totally forgot about those," I said. My heart was still hammering hard from the skateboard antics. I opened up my phone, but the pictures were all too dim to see.

"No luck," I said.

"I don't know," Imani said. "Let's see what Jerrold can do with these."

Five minutes later, the team showed up. "All I have is a burst of blurry photos," I said. "I'm so sorry."

"Oh, no," Jerrold said. "We have so much more."

"What?" I asked.

"Two eyewitnesses who can identify him," he said. "You and Imani."

TWENTY-THREE

The chime of the text alert slowly pulled me from sleep. Where was I? What were all these ruffly blankets? I blinked and recalled that I was on assignment. In the great-aunt's house. I sat up and looked at my phone: eight thirty, and I had a text from Ramón. "Come over for breakfast! My mom's making chorizo omelets . . ."

The team had stayed up late, waiting for a sketch artist to work with me and Imani. I had such a clear picture of John Summer's angry face in my head, but I couldn't quite get the image from my mind to the artist's pencil. Finally, after we changed the cheekbones three times and I still wasn't satisfied, Jerrold called it a night. I compared my sketch to Imani's. The two final sketches didn't look identical, but they were close.

And then we'd looked at a few thousand pictures of known or suspected white supremacists. No luck.

They showed me the surveillance video again. There was no doubt in my mind that the man I saw outside Heather McClelland's door was the same man in the surveillance footage. The way he stood, the way he walked—it was a match.

By morning, I had gotten only a few hours of sleep. "Should I go to the breakfast?" I asked Mom.

"Definitely," Mom said. "See if he might have made contact. Plus, maybe you'll get some decent Mexican food in this town."

When I took a shower, I found all the bruises from the drop-and-roll incident. Elbow, shoulder, hip. It would have been worth it if we had gotten that license plate number.

By nine fifteen, I was setting my skateboard on the porch at Ramón and Kyle's house. I could call them that, right? Ramón and Kyle? Now that I had confessed that I liked Ramón and I knew Kyle wasn't interested in me?

"It smells amazing in here," I said.

Ramón took my hand and squeezed it.

I could feel myself blushing, but I looked down and tried to control it.

Ramón's mom stuck her head into the living room, and Ramón dropped my hand.

"Good morning, ANN-drea," she said. "Glad you could join us."

She disappeared back into the kitchen and Kyle came in, looking even more melancholy than usual.

"Hey, Kyle," I said.

He grunted a half hello and slumped down onto the couch.

"Here's the big ritual," Ramón said. "We watch cartoons until the food is ready around ten. Then we have to go to work."

"Sure," I said. "Sounds good."

Ramón sat in the middle. He held my hand, but low on the couch, almost hidden. It felt weird. My mind flashed back to that look when he had almost kissed me. Was he embarrassed to like me? Was he keeping it a secret? Not only from whoever we ran into on the street but also from his family? Was the almost kiss just last night? Weird. Between confessing to Jerrold and finally seeing the suspect and the delay-the-car skateboard stunt and the police sketch artist and a zillion mugshots, it felt like a month ago.

At Ramón and Kyle's house, the kitchen table was small, fitting only four people, so we sat around the living room. We had plates on our laps for the omelets, which tasted as amazing as they smelled. Suddenly, we heard footsteps on the porch.

"Are you expecting anyone?" Alma asked.

"Did you invite Imani?" I asked.

"She said she was out late," Kyle said.

That was an understatement.

The footsteps seemed to stop on the porch, but no one knocked or rang the bell.

Alma went to the window and looked out through the curtain. "Emily," she said. "I think it's for you."

All eyes followed Emily to the front door.

Heather McClelland was trying to slip an envelope into the mail slot.

"I'm sorry to interrupt," she said. "I was just dropping something off."

"What on earth—" Emily began.

Kyle walked up behind his mother as Heather cut her off. "This is just a letter apologizing," Heather said, handing her the envelope. "I had no idea."

"I'm sorry, too," Kyle's mom said.

"I just wanted you to know that I broke it off with him," Heather said. "He came by last night to try to talk about it, but I was having none of it."

"He's here in town?" Kyle burst out. "He can rush over to your house, but he can't do more than send me an email?" He stormed back through the living room.

"What email?" Emily demanded, going after Kyle as he fled up the stairs.

Heather stood on the porch, facing me, Ramón, and Alma.

"I'm so sorry to stir up old stuff," Heather said. "I'll leave you to your Saturday."

She walked down off the porch, and Alma gently closed the door behind her.

We heard Kyle's door slam upstairs. "Just leave me alone," he yelled, his voice sounding a little muffled from behind his closed door.

"I can't believe he contacted you, and you never told me," Emily said. We could hear her clearly from the upstairs hallway.

"How was I supposed to know you would want me to tell you," Kyle said. "You were never willing to talk about him."

"Fine, we can talk about him!" Emily yelled. "But I'm not doing it through a closed bedroom door."

She stormed back down the stairs. Manners would dictate that I should leave—I should have left after Heather did—but spycraft dictated that I stand perfectly still and quiet. I wanted to hear everything.

A moment later, Kyle came down the stairs. "Tell me what you know," he demanded. "Why did he leave?"

"I don't know," Emily said. "He said he was going off to stay at a hotel to get some space, and I never saw him again."

"Did you ever go to the hotel to try and find him?"

"Of course," she said. "A week later. They said he had left."

"Where'd he go?"

"I have no idea. It was a hotel," his mom said. "Not a college dorm. People just come and go. I met a guy who knew him and said he might have gone off logging up in the Pacific Northwest. There was no way to find him. I got a postcard with an Oregon PO box address at one point, and I wrote him, but he never responded. So I just . . . let it go."

"But you never dated again," Alma said.

"This isn't about that," Emily said.

"It sort of is," Kyle said, his face reddening. "It feels like we've been waiting fifteen years for him to come back."

"Thirteen years!" Emily said.

"But who's counting?" Alma said.

"I just—I just—" Kyle said. His face puckered like he was trying not to cry.

"Hey," Ramón said, looking at me. "We're going out for a walk."

He took my hand and pulled me out the front door.

When we hit the sidewalk, I felt the hot sun on my face. Ramón was right beside me.

"Well," Ramón said. "That was extra."

"I didn't expect a side order of telenovela with my chorizo," I said.

Ramón looked at me strangely.

Had I been too easy with the Spanish?

"You watched telenovelas with your nanny?" he asked.

I nodded. Before we could say anything else, Alma came out the door.

"Ramón, you're going to be late for work," she said, walking over to us. "I'll drive you. I think Kyle is going to call in sick, but you can't afford to miss." She lowered her voice a bit. "I love Emily and Kyle, but you can't let their drama affect your work."

We said our goodbyes, and I skateboarded home.

Later that evening, Jerrold came over. The moment he walked in the door, I knew it was something big. All the other adults on the team were with him.

"What's going on?" I asked.

Jerrold smiled at me. "We got an email response from John Summer."

TWENTY-FOUR

John Summer got our message," Jerrold said. "We emailed from Kyle's school account that Kyle had been in a car accident. Summer doesn't check his messages very often, but we just heard back that he wants to visit Kyle."

"We weren't able to track the message, but Summer says that he's willing to drop everything to be at Kyle's place in 'twenty hours.'"

Mom had pulled up a mapping app on her computer. "The timing checks out," she said to the team. "He could have driven to Colorado and then Montana like he told Heather McClelland. Should we stake out Kyle's house just in case he arrives unexpectedly?"

"Definitely," Jerrold said. "We plan on sending a reply that Kyle's home now but very depressed. We'll say that it would make a difference if John Summer would come." Then Jerrold turned to me. "We want you to be at the house when he gets there so that you can confirm his identity. Where will Kyle be tomorrow?"

"The café for the most part," I said. "Tomorrow is a tournament day. Kyle should be there till around five p.m."

"Right," Mom said. "But we shouldn't try to apprehend Summer at the café. Too many civilians around."

"Okay," I said. "Then you need to time your message so that John Summer will show up tomorrow evening at the house. After the tournament, I'll push for us all to go over to Kyle's."

"Sounds good," Jerrold said. "You can spring for pizza for everyone. Then the pizza delivery kid can be another one of our people."

"Are we going to call in the FBI on this one?" Mom asked.

"I think we have to," Jerrold said. "If we get a second shot at the terrorist, then it's too big a risk not to loop them in."

The next day, I could barely keep my attention on the Triángulo tournament. Imani and I got beaten the first round. My head really wasn't in the game. I kept worrying that John Summer would show up early and that I wouldn't be there to make the ID—or worse, that he would somehow get away.

Ramón and Kyle lasted two rounds. I talked them out of sticking around to watch the third round. I made the "pizza delivery" call (to Jerrold). By the time we got to their house, the delivery guy was there. I made eye contact with him when I signed the fake receipt. He was a young Black man with short dreadlocks.

"The Factory team's all set up," he murmured. "But the FBI isn't in place yet. Apparently, there was a mass shooting in Phoenix, and they diverted some of their agents. Their backup team is on the way now."

I nodded and smiled, like we were chatting about pizza.

He smiled back. "Jerrold said to remind you that the team will wait for your positive ID on Summer," he said.

I nodded again and took the pizza.

A few minutes later, Imani and I were inside Ramón and Kyle's house on the plaid couch, eating pizza and watching their favorite show.

I didn't realize that my eyes kept straying to the door, until Ramón spoke up: "ANN-drea, you wanna watch something different?"

I laughed. "I'm just distracted by the picture of you and Kyle as toddlers," I said, pointing to a photo near the door of a pair of chubby, smiling preschoolers in rompers. Kyle's was blue and Ramón's was green. Ramón was bigger, the age difference clearly showing.

"I know," Imani said. "You all were so cute!"

Ramón rolled his eyes.

Emily walked into the room, and I turned to her. "How old were the boys when that photo was taken?" I asked.

"Let me see . . . they were—" she began, when the doorbell rang, cutting her off. "We're so popular this week." She laughed, walking to the front of the house.

Emily looked through the peephole and gasped.

"Mom," Kyle asked. "Is everything okay?"

"Kyle! Ramón!" Emily said sharply. "Take your friends upstairs."

"Who is it?" Ramón asked.

Emily hesitated for a moment. "Someone who owes me money," she said. "I don't want you all to overhear my language."

The four of us looked at one another.

"Okay, Mom," Kyle said, and he led us upstairs. I brought up the rear, trying to overhear anything I could. Mostly, I just saw Emily standing at the closed door, taking deep breaths as if to prepare herself for an ordeal.

In the upstairs hall, Imani began to wheeze a bit.

We heard the front door open and close again.

"Are you okay, Imani?" I asked.

"I just got startled," she said. "But I don't want to trigger an asthma attack. Can you get my inhaler, ANN-drea? It's in my bag downstairs."

Wow, she was always so smart!

"Of course," I said. "I'll get it now."

I started to walk down the stairs. The front door was closed, but I could see one end of the porch through the window. I could only see a shoe and part of a leg of the man who stood on the porch.

I could see out onto the street. The pizza delivery car was still out front, with the delivery guy pretending to be on his phone.

Across the street were two teen girls kicking a soccer ball back and forth. All three of them were our people.

Everyone was waiting for me to make the ID. If I didn't have time to text, I was supposed to tug my ear when I confirmed it was the terrorist.

I stood behind the door and listened.

"Look, Emily," John Summer was saying. "I just want to see Kyle. To make sure he's okay. To see if there's anything I can do to help."

I looked through the peephole, but all I could see was Emily's broad back. She was nearly as tall as John, and her body was blocking his face.

"Now you want to help?" she asked, throwing up her hands. "*Now?* Unbelievable. Un-freaking-believable."

"Emily, please . . ." His voice was calmer now than it had been when he talked to Heather. More patient. Like he expected she would be upset, like he thought it was reasonable. The night before, he had been more insistent. His voice had a really different tone. Entitled. But after driving so many hours, maybe it wasn't about the emotions. Maybe this was just his exhausted voice.

I crept over to the window on the other side of the door, and I caught a glimpse of the side of John Summer's face. He was clean-shaven now, but the bone structure was right.

"Absolutely not," Kyle's mom said.

I heard the pizza guy's voice crackle in my ear. "FBI has arrived. Two agents in front of the house. Three agents covering the back. They're moving in."

A couple in shades strolled toward the house walking a German shepherd. They looked like a young white hipster couple. They must be FBI.

"Emily, come on!" John Summer said. It was a louder voice, pushing harder now, losing his patience.

I could see a change in his profile. He was angry. His face in a tight scowl.

Suddenly, it felt like the wind had been knocked out of me. Did I see what I thought I saw? When he had been at Heather's, I'd gotten a good look at his angry face when he turned around. At the time, I saw his face full front, and today he was in profile. But no, his expression was totally different. The angry faces didn't match. How was that possible?

I leaned forward to get a clearer look. My hair slipped down over my face, and I tucked it behind my ear to see better.

But then I saw sudden movement in the pizza delivery car.

Wait! What? No! The signal was for me to touch my ear, not tuck my hair. But they had misread it!

"John Summer," the man walking the dog called. He was reaching into his inside pocket.

John turned around and I got a good look at the back of him and his posture for the first time. I had memorized the silhouette of the man at Heather McClelland's apartment. The stance was wrong. The back of the head was wrong. It wasn't him. This man wasn't the same guy I had seen at Heather's! He wasn't the terrorist!

I pressed my hands against the window glass and looked out at the pizza delivery guy, the girls with the soccer ball, the people walking the dog. They had all turned and were facing the house. All of them had their hands at their sides, like they were reaching for holstered weapons.

I shook my head frantically and mouthed, *No!*

For a moment, everything slowed down. I was too late. The guy walking the dog was an FBI agent, and he was already moving in to apprehend John Summer.

But then the agent caught my movement through the window. He looked from me to the man on the porch. Then he broke into a huge smile.

"You don't remember me, John?" he asked, putting away whatever he had been taking out of his pocket.

"We used to drink together at that bar . . . what was it called?"

"The Cowboy Lounge," John Summer said, shaking his head. "I don't remember a lot of what happened there. Sorry. I've been sober for a decade."

"Okay," the FBI guy said. "Then I won't be inviting you for a drink. Nice to see you anyway." He and the female agent began to walk away with the dog, and she already had her phone out.

The girls picked up the soccer ball and walked off. The pizza guy started up the car and drove away.

I got a text from a number I didn't recognize. "You're sure it's not him?"

I was. Wasn't I?

"Imani," I yelled up the stairs. "I can't find it. Can you help me?"

Imani, Kyle, and Ramón came down the stairs.

"You need to look," I said to her pointedly.

"Okay," she said, nodding at me. "I'll look."

She rummaged through her bag while looking out through the window at the porch.

"Did you look thoroughly?" I asked.

"Yeah," she said. "I took a really long look. It's not there."

"You sure?" I asked.

"Positive."

"That's what I thought," I said, feeling relieved.

I texted the team that I was sure. That Imani corroborated.

I got another text. "Plan B: See what you can find out. Clearly, they look very similar. Could he be a relative?"

"Copy that," I texted, and walked over to Kyle. He was looking worriedly at Imani, who was sitting on the couch taking deep breaths.

"I might have misheard," I murmured to Kyle. "But I thought I heard a guy on the street refer to the guy on your porch as John Summer."

"What?" Kyle asked, his head snapping up from Imani. He stomped to the door and opened it wide, letting it bang against the wall.

Alma came in from the kitchen. "What's going on?" she asked.

Ramón looked out through the door at Emily and John. "Is that—?" Ramón asked Kyle. "Your—?"

"Yes," Kyle whispered, his body still frozen.

Emily looked back over her shoulder at all of us. She turned back to John. "Go back in, Kyle," she said, waving a hand behind her. Then she turned to John. "Just go away."

"No!" Kyle said, suddenly regaining his ability to move. He stood in the doorway so his mother couldn't close the door.

"Our family has been fine for the last thirteen

years," Emily said. "We don't need any ghosts coming back to haunt us." She was shaking. Alma came and put an arm around her.

John Summer was standing there. His body was stiff and his mouth was compressed into a line. He was definitely over a decade older than his driver's license picture. I could see that it was the same man from that photo, but not the same man from the surveillance footage. And I could see the lines of Kyle's face in him. The square jaw where Emily's face was narrow. The closer-set eyes, where hers were wide apart.

"He should come in," Kyle said.

John Summer took one tentative step into the room, as if the floor might be made of lava. Just enough to close the door behind him, but no more. He couldn't take his eyes off Kyle.

"Well?" Kyle said. "Aren't you going to give us some sort of explanation?"

"I—" John began. "I've been imagining this day in my mind so many times. And I—"

He took in the rest of us. Alma, in particular. He looked from Emily to Alma.

"This is your n-new—?" he stammered. "You two are—? A family? Are you married?"

"What?" Emily asked. "Are you kidding me?"

Alma laughed. "Spare us your . . . whatever this is," she said. "While you were out writing manifestos about manhood, she was here, raising your son, holding everything together. She and I moved in together because it's so hard for a woman to make it when a man abandons her."

"So you two aren't—?" he sputtered. "What manifestos?"

In that moment, I became 100 percent certain that he wasn't a white supremacist. I was starting to get an idea of what must have happened here.

"Emily showed them to me on the internet," Alma said. "You going on about white men and their burden and how everything is against them. Really? So you just leave your family to fend for themselves, and you think you're the victim here?"

"I never wrote any manifestos," he said. "And you told me to stay out of your lives forever."

"No, we didn't," Emily said. "I would never say that. Kyle's your son. At least, I wouldn't have said it back then. Before I knew what you'd become."

"What are you talking about?" John asked.

"The New Aryan Legion of America?" Emily said. "We saw some of your posts online."

"I n-never . . ." John Summer stammered. "Online? I didn't even have a cell phone till a month ago. It's only been a couple of days since I learned to check messages on it and could answer Kyle's email."

"What email?" Kyle asked.

"Wait," said John. "You're not hurt? What about the car accident?"

"Don't try to change the subject," Emily said as she scrolled on her phone. "This is you, John. It's your picture online." She held up her phone and showed him the page.

"This?" John said. "This is my old driver's license picture. I don't—I never—" He looked up at her. "Is this why you said you never wanted to see me again?"

"I'm telling you, I never said that!" Emily yelled.

"I never wrote any of this!" John yelled back.

"What the hell's happening?" Kyle asked.

"Just calm down, everyone," Ramón said. "There's some kind of mix-up. Or some kind of—"

"Identity theft," I said.

Plan B was in effect.

TWENTY-FIVE

I explained that my mom worked in online security, and she'd taught me about identity theft. I was seriously ad-libbing here, hoping to get him to keep talking, but I was also pretty sure at this point that it was what explained the two John Summers.

"Let's back up," Emily said. "You didn't mean to leave forever?"

"No," John said. "I just—I was immature. I wanted to have a kid, and I imagined it would be . . . I don't know . . . Me and my son playing baseball."

"What if I had been a girl?" Kyle asked. "Or a boy who wasn't the baseball type?"

"That's what I mean," John said. "Immature. A baby doesn't play baseball. A baby needs twenty-four-hour care and attention. I was still a kid myself. Used to your mom paying attention to me. I was jealous."

Kyle looked at his dad with wary eyes. John seemed to be looking through him into the past.

"I couldn't handle the pressure," John said. "The not sleeping. I stormed out to stay at a motel, thinking I would just get a good night's sleep." He ran his fingers through his thinning sandy hair.

"But I ran into a guy I knew from around town," John went on. "And we went out drinking and I lost my wallet, which had all my payday cash in it, and I felt so ashamed. Not only had I run off, but I had lost our rent money. The guy said there was a logging outfit that needed people for short-term work." As John Summer spoke, he shifted his weight from one foot to the other, so he seemed to sort of sway. "It was dangerous, so it paid really well, and I could make the money back in a few days. But it didn't end up being as lucrative as I thought. It took me a couple of weeks. But I finally made the money, and in time to pay the rent."

"Oh," Emily said, sitting up, remembering. "That's why the landlady didn't accept my rent money that day. She said, 'It's been taken care of.' I thought she just felt sorry for me."

"No," John said. "I had paid it. In cash. I had the receipt. After I paid her, I went to my friend. Dave. The one I'd been drinking with. I'd asked him to collect my mail from my PO box while I was gone. He had a letter from you saying that you didn't want to have anything else to do with me. You hated me, and you didn't want to see my face ever again."

"I never sent a letter saying that," Emily said.

"Sometimes identity thieves do things like that," I said. As things got increasingly personal, I needed to justify my continued presence.

"It sounds like he was part identity thief, part con man," Ramón said.

"Yeah," I said. "And I would question whether you really lost your wallet that first night you two went drinking or if he stole it. Did the two of you look alike?"

"I guess we did," he said. "We could be cousins. Brothers, maybe."

Having seen the fake John Summer, I agreed.

"I went back to the logging operation for another month," John said. "I made enough to pay three months' rent. I went to the old apartment in Phoenix just before rent was due. I had these fantasies of being the hero. I'd swoop in with a bunch of money, a dozen roses, and a brand-new tricycle for Kyle. I'd declare myself back, and my gifts would win you over, Emily."

"What happened?" Ramón asked.

"They were gone," John said. "No forwarding address. I was— I just— That's when it sank in. I had screwed it up forever. No knot of cash and dozen roses were gonna fix it."

"Where did you go?" Kyle asked.

"I went back to logging," John said. "I found a safer outfit. It didn't pay as much, but I didn't need a lot of money anymore. I was just . . . in survival mode . . . I didn't think I would ever . . . I searched for you, from time to time, but it hurt too much every time I failed. You didn't want me, anyway, and I convinced myself that maybe you were better off. But then I saw the photo of Kyle in the paper. And I sent the email last year. And when you never got back to me, I thought I had ruined that, too."

"He emailed you a year ago?" Emily turned to Kyle accusingly. "You kept this from me for a whole year?"

"I needed to figure it out for myself," Kyle said.

"I had lost hope," John said. "But then I got an email from you—"

"What?" Emily said. "You replied to him?"

"No," Kyle said. "I never did."

I butted in. "My mom always says that with an identity thief in the mix, it can be hard to know what communication is real and what's fake."

"But you're together now," Imani said. "And it sounds like you all didn't really want to stay apart. And so now you can talk everything out."

"You didn't want me to stay gone all this time?" John Summer asked.

"No," Emily said. "I wanted you back. We both did."

That was when John Summer lost it. The tall,

awkward logger started bawling. Kyle was crying, too. And Emily.

I looked over at the wall. There was a picture of a smiling dog that Ramón had drawn as a little kid. He spelled it "dag."

"Come on," Alma said. "We should go clean up the kitchen."

I went with her, Imani, and Ramón, and we did the dishes without speaking for a while.

"Whoa," Imani finally said. "That's the craziest story."

"I can't help but wonder if I should have done something differently," Alma said. "I didn't encourage Emily to look harder. Maybe I should have."

"You can't blame yourself," Ramón said. "You were a young widow and a new immigrant. You had just gotten an eviction notice. You were just trying to survive."

"But if I hadn't encouraged Emily to move to a cheaper apartment out here in Carson, she would've been there when he came back."

"John said it himself," Imani said. "He kept his wife in the dark for three months and didn't tell her he was coming back. He expected her to sit around waiting to be rescued. Of course she made other plans."

"You had no way of knowing," Ramón said.

"Only one person is responsible for this mess," I said. "And that's the identity thief."

"Good thing you were here," Ramón said.

I smiled and handed him a dish to dry.

Things had settled down in the living room. The dishes were done. Kitchen table cleared. Floor swept.

John was sitting down now, holding his body stiffly in the plaid armchair. Kyle and Emily sat together on the couch.

"I can't believe all this time I thought you'd abandoned us," Emily said, "and you thought we didn't want you back."

"It was my fault," John said. "I never should've left in the first place. I should've talked to you, instead of cooking up these ridiculous hero fantasies. I'm so sorry."

"I have a question," I said. "Was it Dave who suggested that you play the hero?"

John frowned. "Well . . . I don't know . . . originally?" he said. "We were . . . Hey! Now that you mention it . . . Yeah, he did."

"That's how identity thieves manipulate people," I said. "We should call the authorities."

"I'll call the police," Emily said.

"Even better," I said. "My mom knows someone at the FBI who specializes in this kind of thing."

Everyone looked impressed.

"Let me make a call," I said, hoping I could pull this off.

I went out on the porch and called Jerrold to explain exactly what had been going on.

"I'm so sorry about the false ID," I said.

"No need for apologies," he said. "You've done great."

When I went back in, everyone was smiling and laughing.

"There's one thing I don't understand though," Emily said. "Why did the identity thief write to you from Kyle's account?"

I sent Jerrold a quick text. "They're looking at the email from Kyle's account."

"I was wondering that, too," Kyle said.

"Let me pull up the email," John said. "I figured out the email thing a couple days ago, just so I could check for any more messages from you. But my fingers are so big, I keep pressing the wrong thing . . ."

"It's because you're trying to check it in the web browser," Kyle said. "You have to set up the email in the mail app on the phone to make it easier. Here . . ."

It took them about ten minutes to get his email app working. Imani and I glanced at each other across the living room.

I held my breath as they opened the message.

"This is obviously a phishing scam," Kyle said. "See? They say I'm sick and you need to click this link to send money."

"Really?" John asked. "How did I miss this the first time?"

"Yeah," Kyle said. "And this second one says I'm depressed and you should click the link to donate."

"I just—wow," John said. "I totally thought it said to come see you."

Emily laughed. "I'll bet this is the first time anyone is glad to be the victim of a phishing scam," she said. "If they hadn't sent you that fake email, you never would have come."

TWENTY-SIX

In the FBI office in Phoenix, Kyle's dad—the real John Summer—sat in the interrogation room, a grim little box with harsh lighting. Mom and I stood on the other side of the two-way mirror. John still had on the blue button-down shirt he'd been wearing at the house, but by now he had a bit of reddish stubble on his face. He held his body even more stiffly in the FBI desk chair and blinked nervously.

John recounted the story he told his family. The agent showed him the sketches the artist had made for Imani and me.

John Summer nodded. Yes. That was Dave.

By then we knew that "Dave" had used John Summer's ID and the thumbprint from his driver's license. He had used his identity for several of his online activities posting white supremacist content. We didn't know much more about Dave. Only two sketches of what he looked like, two eyewitnesses, and the fact that he was allegedly in Las Vegas when Heather texted him. The agent asked if John Summer could remember if Dave had given him a last name. He couldn't remember. But none of us were particularly disappointed. It would probably have proven to be fake as well.

The next days were a blur. Kyle was no longer the surveillance target, but we needed to stay in town to keep an eye on Heather McClelland, in case she got back in touch with Dave. Imani and I were the only ones who could identify the terrorist, so we were on call.

Jerrold had a team of operatives following Heather around all day and staking out her apartment all night, looking to see if she interacted with anyone who fit the description. Once, we got a call in the early afternoon and had to rush out to the mall to see if we could identify the guy she'd been talking with. One member of the team had continued following Heather, while another followed a tall, blond guy.

It wasn't the terrorist.

The next day, I had instructions to touch base with Kyle and Ramón. Just routine contact with the subjects as our team changed gears.

My heart beat faster as I picked up my phone to call Ramón. I'd pretended to be sick so that I could look through mug shots rather than spend time at school. I made my voice sound hoarse, but we managed to chat.

"Guess what?" Ramón said. "Kyle's parents are thinking about getting back together."

"Oh my God," I said. "Wow."

"I heard Emily say she wasn't ready to have him move in or anything," Ramón said.

"Move in?" I said. "How would he fit?"

"That's the thing," Ramón said. "You haven't really seen the whole house. But it's not that big. Kyle and I could share a bedroom, and his parents could have a bedroom, and my mom could sleep in the other bedroom that I'm in now . . ."

I could visualize all of it, but he didn't know that. "But how would that be fair to your mom?" I asked.

"I agree," Ramón said. "Maybe Mami and I would move, and they'd have the house."

"How is that any more fair?" I asked.

"Not so much about fair," Ramón said. "But we can't afford the place by ourselves. Kyle's family could."

"Why couldn't you all move into a much bigger place?" I asked.

"We could," Ramón said. "But Emily is like, 'Let's just date for a while and see how it goes.'"

"'Date'?" I said. "How can you date someone you were married to and had a child with fifteen years ago?"

"I'll never understand adults," Ramón said. "But speaking of dating—"

I faked a coughing fit. We were nearly wrapping up the case. I didn't want him to bring up the liking-each-other thing if I was going to be leaving soon. "I'm sorry," I said. "You were saying?"

He started to speak again, and I coughed again.

"You don't sound good," he said. "I heard this flu is really nasty, even though it's not the usual flu season. You should go rest."

"I guess—" I coughed a bunch. "I guess you're right. I'll call you when I'm better."

TWENTY-SEVEN

My brother gets on my nerves, but I never realized how much I missed him until I was alone with Mom. From the time he had learned to walk, I had complained about how my little brother was always toddling after me, but it meant that when I was bored, I could always say, "Hey, Carlos, let's . . ." whatever. Build a fort in the living room. Throw a ball in the yard. Play cards. Bake cookies. Something. After we realized John Summer wasn't the real terrorist, our operation went into limbo. I sat around the house all day while Mom worked overtime analyzing the intelligence they had gathered. I texted Imani, but she said she was in Kreyol language immersion class, because her family might be needed for an operation in Haiti. Mostly I was bored. And lonely. And, to be honest, I felt like sort of a failure. My first mission. And we had hit a dead end.

But four days after my conversation with Ramón, we finally got a break in the case. Mom had been monitoring several credit cards and email addresses the terrorist sometimes used, and found that he'd paid for a bus ticket and sent a message to a chemical weapon maker to meet him on the way to "Esdee."

"What on earth is 'Esdee'?" I asked.

"It's a paint company in India," Mom said. But the frown between her eyebrows meant she wasn't satisfied with that answer.

"You can't really get to India on the bus," I said.

She shook her head. "Is it slang for anything in your generation?"

"You're asking me?" I said. "I've only gone to regular school for a few weeks."

"Apparently, it's also a first name," she said. "But I can't imagine saying 'See you in such and such person's name.'"

Esdee? Esdee? I ran the word silently over and over in my mouth.

"What if it's not a proper name?" I said. "What if it's initials: SD?"

She nodded. "Could be South Dakota," she said.

"Or San Diego," I said.

"Let's check in with Jerrold."

• • •

Jerrold verified that the amount of money for the bus ticket would get him from Las Vegas to San Diego, but wouldn't be nearly enough to get him to South Dakota.

"Are you covering the bus stations?" I asked.

"Las Vegas has several bus stations, and so does San Diego," he said. "We have a few people looking out in both cities, but it's a long shot. We don't have the FBI's resources."

"Don't even get me started . . ." Mom began.

"Our contact keeps trying," Jerrold said. "But the higher-ups say he doesn't have enough evidence."

Which, of course, did get Mom started. "It's so outrageous," she fumed. "We do ninety-nine percent of the work. We're only asking them to show up for the nab. Everybody in intelligence knows you don't get your guy on the first try. Sometimes not even on the second. They understand that for every other type of crime. But somehow when it's white supremacists, it's too much work unless it's basically effortless."

Our team went over the information again on a video-conference call with Jerrold.

Imani and I sat beside each other on the couch. Mom sat in the armchair. The coffee table was covered in files.

"We have a possible city," Jerrold said. "A date range in July, and we know it's a white supremacist attack. What are some possible targets?"

"It could be a San Diego Padres baseball game," Mom said.

"Or a professional soccer game," I said.

"Soccer?" Imani said. "San Diego has professional soccer?"

"It's very popular among the Latin American community," I said, a little defensively. I had played soccer all my life and thought of it as a major sport. "I think it could be a target."

"There's plenty of activity at the San Diego's Del Mar racetrack," Imani said.

"There are a lot of Fourth of July celebrations," Mom said.

"I could see that," Jerrold said. "Sometimes patriotism and xenophobia go hand in hand."

"There are a bunch of special events in the area," Mom said. "County fair . . . San Diego Gay Pride."

"White supremacists don't like the rainbow," Jerrold said.

"And there are landmarks that might be a target," Mom said. "Like that huge, new Power of Africa exhibit at the San Diego Zoo."

"We can't narrow it down quite enough," Jerrold said. "It could be any of these."

"Do we have anything else to go on?" I asked.

Mom sighed. "I haven't wanted to give you all his manifesto materials," she said. "It's—it's pretty scary stuff. But our team has been poring over it for months now. Maybe it's time for some new eyes. Jerrold?"

"Sounds like our best play," he said.

We signed off from the videoconference. Mom went to the study to get the printouts.

As we waited for her to get back, I turned to Imani. "Have you read any of this stuff before?" I asked.

"Nope," she said. "My mom was like yours. She didn't want me to see any of the white nationalist propaganda unless it was absolutely necessary. She said it gave her nightmares. And she's a really experienced spy who's seen a lot."

Five minutes later, Mom dumped a huge pile of papers in front of Imani and me.

"Divide and conquer?" she asked.

"Sure," I said. I picked up the top page, which was the email they'd recently intercepted. Just five words. "Meetup en route to Esdee." I looked at everything on the page. The date. The time. The email addresses. From n8TrØl8zØ@xmail.com to airmaster@xmail.com.

His email looked like a random string of letters and numbers, like a password. But wait. Why would he randomize the email address? It wasn't encrypted or encoded.

Imani saw me sit up and jot something down. "You find something?" she asked.

"I don't know," I said.

I put the letters into all caps to make it easier on the eyes. N8TRØL8ZØ.

"Neight-ro-leight-zo?" she asked.

Then I saw it. My eyes got wide and I yelled out, "Naturalezo!"

"From Triángulo?" she asked.

"What are you talking about?" Mom asked. "That card game?"

"It's more than a card game," I said. "It's taking over everything in the world of nerds: games, comics, and there's a video game coming out and a movie later this year. It's gonna be the big thing this year at—"

Imani and I looked at each other, wide-eyed, and said it at the same time.

"San Diego ComxCon!"

"It's in July," I added.

"Se konsa!" Imani said, grinning. "It means 'that's right' in Haitian Kreyol."

Mom smiled. "Let the young people lead the way," she said.

"Naturalezo is the supervillain in the present time and an enslaver in the seventeenth century," Imani said. "He would be the big hero for Team Racism."

"Can you give me a list of other characters or words that would be part of that ideology?" Mom asked.

"Sure," Imani said, and started jotting them down on a legal pad.

"Do you think this is it?" I asked.

"It's our best lead so far," Mom said. "I'm going to go back through all his materials and see if I can't search out these keywords."

"Fingers crossed," I said. "I'll update Jerrold."

"Should we feel relieved?" Imani asked.

"Not yet," Mom said.

But as I called Jerrold, I already felt relieved. I was glad that I didn't have to go through all those manifestos by the white supremacists.

Twenty minutes later, Jerrold had joined us at the great-aunt's house, AKA headquarters.

He walked into the room and, as always, I felt reassured. His voice was deep and calm but optimistic. He always looked the same: neatly cut hair, rimless glasses, and a three-piece suit. The shade of the fabric varied slightly from navy to brown to gray to deep forest green. Today it was charcoal, with a brick-red tie.

Mom showed him the file, where she had identified more than one hundred references to Triángulo in the communications they had intercepted. She had also found a ton of controversy online, particularly on social media, about what some were calling a woman-of-color takeover of ComxCon. Certain white male corners of the internet were bemoaning this fact, while other communities were celebrating.

Now that there were four of us, Mom had moved

the operation to the kitchen table. We had four laptops open, and the stack of files had grown even taller.

"It makes sense as a target for these white extremists," Jerrold said.

"An estimated 135,000 people attend that gathering every year," Mom said. "A chemical weapon could kill everyone inside the Con—attendees, staff, presenters—and maybe even affect people outside. Depending on the size and strength of the weapon, he might kill—or at least harm—up to a quarter million people."

"It's settled," Jerrold said. "Imani and Andréa, start planning your cosplay outfits."

"Their what?" Mom asked.

"Their costumes for ComxCon," Jerrold said.

"Are you kidding, Jerrold?" Mom asked. "It's much too dangerous for them to go."

Jerrold looked from me and Imani to my mom. He took a deep breath and settled himself in his chair.

"Bárbara, you need to stop thinking as a mother and think as a spy on a team," he said quietly. "Imani and Andréa are the only ones who can identify him."

"What about Heather? She could do a much better job of identifying him. Plus, we could use her as bait to attract him."

"You know they haven't had any more contact," Jerrold said. His voice was calm but direct. "And we can't trust her. With barely a week to try to get her to operate on our behalf? You know there's no contest between a civilian sometime-girlfriend and an experienced operative."

"'Experienced operative'?" Mom said, her voice rising. "She's fourteen, Jerrold. I gave permission for her to participate in this operation—despite my objections after what happened in Puerto Rico—because you promised me that she would only be at a high school, befriending an estranged son. Not running around a convention that is the target of a terrorist attack, trying to find and confront the terrorist. Who's armed with a freaking *chemical weapon*."

"Bárbara," Jerrold said, his voice still calm. "Andréa has shown herself to be smart and capable. We may be talking about a quarter million lives at stake. She needs to go."

"She's standing right here," I said. "And she can speak for herself."

"Actually, you can't," Mom said. "Our contract with Jerrold doesn't supersede my authority as a mother to consent or not consent to your activities as a minor."

Jerrold's mouth contracted into a tight circle. Then he took another breath and his face relaxed.

"You're saying I need my mom's permission to do this?" I asked. "What? Is there a slip that says, 'My child blank has my permission to stop a terrorist attack at ComxCon. I'll be packing her a bag lunch'? Mom, you need to see reason here. This is an important mission with thousands of lives at stake. You and Papi chose this spy life for our family, and now we're in it. All of us. I'm not a baby anymore, and you need to let me see this through."

"Cariño, I respect your developing spycraft, but it's just too dangerous," Mom said. "I—"

"No, Mami," I said. "If you really do respect me, you'll let me do my job."

"What about my job?" she asked, her eyes blazing. "It's my job to protect you—"

Now my eyes were blazing, too. Why couldn't she see how patronizing this was? I couldn't stand to listen to it for one more minute, so I stood up.

"Where are you going?" Mom asked.

"To pack, obviously," I spat. "We're going back to LA. If I can't go to ComxCon, the operation's over."

"It's not—" Mom began, but I cut her off.

"Do I get to say goodbye to the two kids I was nannying?" I asked. "Or do Ramón and Kyle just get to wonder where I went?"

"Andréa!" my mom said sharply. "The thing you don't understand—"

Jerrold held up a hand. "Let her go, Bárbara."

I went upstairs to our fake bedroom and slammed the door. I'd never moved in for real.

I didn't pack, because there was nothing to pack. As part of my spy training, I kept everything in the suitcase, except the clothes on my back.

I threw myself down on the bed and fumed.

Through the slammed door, I heard voices. Mom, loud and shrill. Then Jerrold, a low rumble in between her outbursts. I couldn't make out any of the words.

There was a knock on my door.

"Go away, Mom," I said.

"It's Imani."

"Oh," I said. "Come in."

"Hey," she said. She closed the door behind her and sat down on the edge of the bed.

"How do you do it?" I asked. "Go from being an ordinary teenager who needs her parents' permission to go on a field trip to making life-and-death decisions in an instant?"

"I don't know," Imani said. "It's not easy. I just . . . I really . . . I guess I've learned that our parents are spies, but they're also parents. They make mistakes. Sometimes they're so sure they know what's right for me, and they're just totally wrong. Sometimes they're right. And you never know who was right until after it all shakes out."

"What am I supposed to do?" I asked. "Just let her steamroll over me for this decision?"

"She's scared," Imani said. "What would you do with a subject who was scared but you needed them to do something brave? You're asking a mother to agree to risk her daughter's life."

We were quiet for a minute. Through the door, I couldn't hear my mom or Jerrold anymore.

"What would I do if she was a subject?" I asked. "I'd handle her."

"So would I," Imani said.

I walked down the wooden stairs. The work stuff was still on the kitchen table, but everyone sat in the living room: Jerrold on a kitchen chair, a picture of calm, and Mom on the couch with her arms folded across her chest. Imani had already returned to the living room and was sitting in the armchair.

I walked into the living room. "Mom," I said. "I'd like to make my case."

Her eyes were red. Had she been crying?

"Okay," she said tightly.

"You took an oath," I said. "You weren't much older than me—"

"I was nineteen," she said.

"Please don't interrupt," I said. "I'm making my case. You were a teenager, and you knew this organization's cause was worth fighting for. You decided to dedicate your life to the cause, and that meant putting yourself in dangerous situations."

"You don't understand," she said. "I didn't grow up like you. In a nice house. Visiting hotels on vacation. I lost both my parents. I grew up in the roughest barrio. Taking risks as a spy was nothing to me. Your dad was the same." She shook her head. "When we started a family, we stopped taking the riskiest assignments.

Yes, there's always danger, but we minimized it. It's not fair when you have a family."

"Life's not fair," I said. "Isn't that what Dad told us so many times? It's not fair that this man has been able to get his hands on a chemical weapon. It's not fair that the FBI—the organization that's supposed to be fighting guys like this—would be all over it if his name was Abdul Mohammed or LeRon Johnson or even Ernesto Sánchez. But when the suspect is named John Summer and has sandy hair and blue eyes, we can't get them to use the full force of their institution to find him and stop him. Which is why our organization exists. You're worried about your daughter. I get that. I'm worried about the quarter million people in and around that convention center. All those daughters, and more young women of color than ever before."

Mom's eyes were filling up.

"I can't make you give permission for me to go," I said. "Yes, there's the possibility that I could get hurt or even killed. I can live with that. What I can't live with is the idea of playing it safe when I'm one of two operatives who can identify this man, and I could be the difference that saves these lives. Can you live with that?"

"It's an impossible choice!" Mom said. She was definitely crying now. "When I was a teenager, I was reckless. I didn't respect my own life and safety. When we had you and your brother, we vowed to protect you. We stopped risking our own lives like that."

"I'm not you," I said. "I'm not reckless. I bring everything you taught me to the field. I'm a good agent."

"She is, Bárbara," Jerrold said.

Mom was on her feet, pacing.

"If you don't let me go and anything happens, I'll never forgive myself," I said. "And you'll never forgive yourself."

"If anything happens to you, I'll never forgive myself." She was standing right by Jerrold now, and she turned to him, eyes blazing.

Before she could say anything to him, I jumped in. "You have to protect me by being an agent on my team," I said. "Not by being a parent who forbids me to go."

Mom turned to Jerrold and he nodded. She balled her fist, like she was going to punch him, but then she sort of doubled over and started sobbing. Jerrold stood and supported her weight with an arm across her belly. She hung off his arm like a rag doll, the emotion so heavy, she couldn't even hold herself up.

She cried for a couple minutes. I stood there, stunned. I had never seen her like this. And then she just stopped. She took a ragged breath and stood up, her jaw tight. "Okay," Mom said with a sharp nod. "I give my permission."

Jerrold released her, and she sat down on the couch. He sat beside her. With a shaking hand, she reached for her coffee cup on the end table.

"Good handling," Imani whispered to me.

I could only nod as I sat down on Mom's other side. I should have felt jubilant. I had gotten Mom to take me seriously as an agent. But I was still shaken by her breakdown. And I was going to a huge convention to face an armed terrorist. I felt overwhelmed with conflicting emotions: some determination and pride, because I had gotten Mom to stop treating me like a little kid. But that was just it. I wasn't a little kid anymore. My mom wasn't going to be able to keep me safe. Just as I had asked—no, demanded—to be treated like an adult, it was dawning on me that my parents wouldn't be able to protect me in the same ways they had.

TWENTY-EIGHT

Eighteen hours later, I was dry-eyed and focused. After our emotional meeting, I had done what I could to prepare myself, starting with a brutal calisthenic workout and stretching, and then to bed, where I slept well and woke up feeling sharp.

Our team was meeting again at the great-aunt's house, where we were subdued and somber. Jerrold sat at the table with a laptop. Across from him, Mom was still working her way through a stack of files. Imani and I sat on the couch, looking at ComxCon info, both online and in hard copy.

On the one hand, we had a good idea of the target time and location, as well as a plan to apprehend the terrorist. On the other hand, we would be looking for a thirty-something white guy at ComxCon. How would we be able to find the terrorist when so many people there also answered to his description, especially if a lot of them would be dressed up and wearing masks?

I asked Jerrold as much.

"Actually," he said, "he probably will wear a mask since our intelligence tells us he'll be using a chemical weapon. Look for a loner. One guy. His mask would likely be a real gas mask."

"Convenient," Imani said.

"We're just going to wait around until ComxCon next week?" I asked.

"Not exactly," Jerrold said. "The one who can do the best job of identifying the terrorist is John Summer."

"The one who knows him best is Heather McClelland," Imani said. "It's been years since John Summer has seen Dave."

"True," Jerrold said. "But they were friends for a while back then. He'd be able to make the ID. And we need someone whom we can convince to come along. We don't have an in with Heather, but it would be natural for you to invite Kyle and Ramón, and we think we can get them to bring Kyle's dad."

"Isn't it too dangerous to bring them along?" I asked.

Jerrold sighed. "Believe me, it's not my preference," he said. "But the FBI keeps raising the bar on the kind of evidence they need to detain and prosecute these guys. A positive ID from the man whose identity he stole? Plus two teen agents as eyewitnesses? That would probably do the trick."

"But still," I said. "They would have no idea what they were walking into."

"We will take every possible measure to keep them safe," Jerrold said. "To keep everyone safe. If it comes down to it, I will call in a bomb threat, and they will evacuate the entire place."

"Let's hope it doesn't come to that," Imani said.

"But meanwhile," I said, "am I supposed to recruit John Summer?"

"No," Mom said, pointing to herself. "Barbara Burke will recruit him."

"Can we use this opportunity to share our true identities?" I asked. I was so sick of pretending to be white.

Jerrold shook his head. "We can't afford to arouse any suspicions," he said. "You two showed up in town at the most random of times, clearly saying you're one thing and then suddenly becoming another? These kids are very astute. They'll start asking questions. The Factory maintains a strict protocol of keeping our identities secret from start to finish of any operation."

I was disappointed. The idea of telling Ramón I was Latina was really appealing. But the job came first.

"We need you to reestablish contact with Kyle and Ramón," Jerrold said. "You'll need to suggest that you all go to the Con."

"Okay," I said. "Can we take separate cars to San Diego?"

"Definitely," Mom said. "Our 'car' will be a plane."

A weekend away with Imani, Kyle, Ramón, Kyle's estranged dad, and my mother pretending to be white? That shouldn't be awkward at all.

I went to Ramón and Kyle's house after school, and Ramón answered the door.

"You're finally over your flu?" he asked.

"Yeah." I fake coughed a couple of times. "I'm so glad to be better."

"Still not back in school, though?" he asked.

"I need a lot of rest," I said. In fact, we were all working overtime, trying to get more information about the terrorist. I was looking through screen after screen of photographs of different white guys who had attended the last three ComxCons. It was mind-numbing, but I had to stay alert. It was such a relief to talk to an actual human—one who was easier on the eyes.

"Hey, ANN-drea," Kyle said, coming into the living room. It was so jarring to hear my cover name again. Jerrold and Mom and even Imani had been calling me Andréa.

"Hey, Kyle," I said. "I'm glad I have both of you here. I was wondering . . . I mean . . . Imani and I were hoping . . . Well. My mom has an extra pair of passes to ComxCon!"

"In San Diego?" Ramón asked. "Holy crap!"

"You guys wanna go?"

"Are you kidding?" Kyle asked.

"What about work?" Ramón asked.

"We have a week to ask for the time off," Kyle said.

"How do we get there?"

"We won't all fit in my mom's car," I said.

"Can we take the bus?" Kyle asked.

"Not alone," Ramón said.

"Maybe my mom would drive us," Kyle said.

"That won't work," Ramón said. "Your mom hates long drives, and my mom needs to work here in town." I breathed a sigh of relief. We'd been counting on Ramón's mom having to work, but if Kyle's mom had been available, she might not have been excited about bringing his dad. Would that have been awkward for the two of them? This made my job easier.

"What about your dad?" I asked.

"My . . . yeah . . ." Kyle said. "He's been wanting to—you know—do some bonding. This could totally work!"

"Can you all come over for dinner?" I asked. "My mom is in sales, and I think she could sell your parents on this."

"I thought your mom worked on identity theft stuff," Kyle said.

"She sells security software for computer systems," I said. "To prevent identity theft." It was a mouthful, but I'd practiced it several times until it rolled easily off my tongue.

"Dinners are hard for my mom," Ramón said. "She's been taking a night class."

"My mom's free," Kyle said.

"Your dad probably doesn't have any plans," Ramón added.

"If both my parents are on board, we can probably convince your mom," Kyle said.

"Probably," Ramón said. "As long as it's free."

"'Both my parents,'" Kyle said, shaking his head. "When has that phrase ever come out of my mouth?"

TWENTY-NINE

Mom and I sat at the dining room table. Mom wore a salmon-colored cashmere sweater, slacks, and a string of pearls. The color worked with her skin tone. She looked like a white TV mom. I did my best to look the part of the white TV daughter. A lavender tee with pale blue jeans. We matched the house's pastel decor.

The doorbell rang, and I opened the door to Kyle, his parents, and Ramón.

"Barbara Burke," my mother said, holding out her hand.

"My mom can come by after her class," Ramón said.

"Lovely," my mom said. "We'll save her dessert."

Emily remarked that the house was nice. I attributed it to my decision to put away more of the big-eyed animals.

"It's my great-aunt's place," I said as I brought out a tray of iced tea.

"It's mint. All herbal," Mom said. "My system can't handle caffeine." Which was the biggest lie. Her Puerto Rican family had given her Café Bustelo coffee from the time she was a toddler. My mom drank it all day, and it didn't seem to affect her.

Emily was smiling more than I'd ever seen, and John Summer was letting his beard grow back out. Kyle sat between them on the couch and beamed.

We made small talk until it was time for dinner, then everyone sat down.

"Smells delicious, Mrs. Burke," Ramón said.

"Thank you," Mom said as she brought out a big pan of meat loaf, one of Barbara Burke's specialties. I followed with a wooden bowl of Caesar salad.

Everyone served themselves. "This is so good," Emily said. "It's been a while since I had homemade meat loaf."

"My pleasure. I really appreciate all of you coming over tonight," Mom said. "As ANN-drea may have told you, I'm in sales. Our firm does ComxCon every year, and I usually leave her in Los Angeles with her father. Stepfather. But this year, it's not possible, because of the separation—I don't know if ANN-drea has told you we're getting a divorce—and now she's passionately into this triangle game and wants to come. I need another adult I trust to chaperone the children."

"Children?" I asked.

"Kids," Mom said. "Young people. Future of America." She waved her hand dismissively. "You know what I mean."

"Our family is in its own little . . . shake-up, I guess you could call it," Emily said. "John and I have been . . . separated for a long time. The timing is good for him to do something with Kyle and to get to know Ramón. They've been like brothers all these years."

"It could be really great," John said.

"I have an extra pair of passes," Mom said.

"I can buy my own ticket," John said. "Are the hotels all booked?"

Mom waved his comment away. "My company has a block of hotel rooms," she said. "There's usually an extra."

"That'd be amazing," John said.

"Yeah," Mom said. "You'd just need to get there and back and feed yourselves."

"That's so generous," Emily said.

"It's more of a mutual aid situation," Mom said. "I need to work. I'm not going to leave ANN-drea here without adult supervision. Or let her run loose at ComxCon—not that she generally gets into trouble, but . . . the world being what it is . . . I'm glad you all are open to the idea."

"More than open," Kyle said, his eyes bright. "I think we can call it a yes!"

• • •

Later that night, some of us went out to celebrate. The town always did a big celebration on the Fourth of July, and they had a fireworks show after sundown.

Ramón and I sat on the side of a hill to watch the fireworks. Kyle and his dad had hiked up to a higher point famous for having the best view; you had to get there, like, an hour early. Ramón and I were holding hands, discreetly again, but with just the two of us together, it was pretty clear that we were . . . on a date or something.

The fireworks show was beautiful. I knew they were terrible for the environment, but I didn't let that knowledge spoil the dazzle of the lights and colors.

On the way home, Ramón held my hand for real, even when we walked past a group of Latine kids. "Hey, Ramón," one of them called.

"Hey, Nestor," he called back. He didn't stop or let go of my hand.

When we got to my house, he looked me right in the face. "ANN-drea," he said. "I know we've been sort of casually hanging out. And I've been sort of . . . shy about . . . or just sort of awkward because . . . I mean, I really like you."

My heart was beating fast. I couldn't fake a coughing fit this time, but I didn't want to interrupt him.

"But this town is so . . . divided. And I couldn't totally

imagine you and me . . . you know . . . together . . . but then I think about going someplace like San Diego . . . and suddenly there seem to be more possibilities . . . And I realized that I didn't want to let what other people think get in the way. Anyways, I guess . . . I was wondering . . . I was hoping . . . that you'd be my girlfriend?"

I smiled at him. Did he really ask that? Was this really happening? "Yes," I said, grinning. "I'd like that a lot."

He swallowed hard, blinking at me in the soft glow of the sunset. "I never thought a girl like you would like a geeky Latino guy like me," he said. "And since we're going to San Diego ComxCon, in the year of Triángulo, where there will literally be thousands of geeky Latino guys, I thought I'd better make it official ahead of time, in case that's, like, your type—"

And then he couldn't talk, because I had leaned forward to kiss him. His mouth was startled at first, but then he kissed back, and there was a moment when it was like floating. I didn't worry about my mom opening the door or about who might be watching.

Which turned out to be a mistake.

"Hey!" An angry male voice interrupted the moment. "What the hell are you doing?"

The two of us looked up, disoriented.

"Get away from her," one of them said.

What the heck was his problem? But then he added a racist insult, and I understood.

There were three white guys. Young adults, maybe. They looked drunk.

"Freakin' beaner," another one said. "Let that white girl alone."

"I don't want any trouble," Ramón said.

We tried to back toward the house, but one of them circled behind us.

Reflexively, I shifted my feet to a fighting stance. I was about to raise my fists in front of my face, but I thought better of it. As spies, we weren't supposed to attract any attention.

"If you didn't want any trouble, you shouldn't have put your hands on one of our women," he said.

"Please," I said, making my voice sound high and scared. "Just leave us alone."

The three of them began to close in. I wasn't sure what to do. I knew how to defend myself from multiple attackers. I had studied five different martial arts systems. I had a lip gloss that turned into a knife. But I was supposed to be a high school student, not a spy.

"Back off," Ramón said, and he put up his fists in front of his face.

I looked from the guys to the house. How could I get us out of this? We were right in front of our headquarters. I could fight them, but what if I broke a bone or gave one of them a concussion? They could come back and make trouble before the operation was over. Or what if they called the police? Would cops come sniffing around Mom and me and get suspicious? Would they dig into our cover story? Or worse yet, would there be cruisers looking for Ramón on his way home?

"Leave me and my girlfriend alone," Ramón said.

"'Girlfriend'?" one of the guys said. "I wonder how much your white girlfriend will like you with all your teeth missing?"

"This Fourth of July, we're gonna teach you the real meaning of America," another guy said.

I needed to do something.

"We'll teach you to stick to girls of your own dirty race," the guy in front said, and lunged toward us. He had something in his hand.

I threw myself in front of Ramón. "But I am!" I blurted out. "I'm Latina. I'm just light. My dad's Mexican."

"You're lying," the closest guy said.

"No. Te juro," I said. "Soy latina y orgullosa."

The guys all recoiled.

"Freakin' secret Mexicans," one of the guys spat. "Go back to your side of town."

I didn't say that I lived on this side of town, that we were standing in front of my house. I grabbed Ramón's hand and we ran. They chased us for what felt like a mile.

The guys were taller and had longer legs. But they had probably been drinking. Maybe ten blocks down, we lost them.

Ramón and I were both breathing hard. I was sweating and wiped my forehead.

"Are you okay?" I asked.

Ramón shook his head. "What you said back there," he said slowly. "It's true, isn't it? Your dad's Mexican?"

We stood under a streetlight, and he squinted at me. "I can see it," he said. "Your eyes. And your—your hair."

I reached up and, with the sweat from running, the roots of my hair were starting to curl.

"The guy didn't cut you, did he?" I asked.

Ramón's face was hurt, angry. "That jerk didn't cut me," Ramón said. "You did. How could you?"

"How could I what?"

"How could you backstab your people?" he asked. "'Latina y orgullosa'? You're not proud. You've been acting white this whole time. When I called you a white girl, you didn't deny it. How could you hide who you are, and then think it would be all fine and dandy with me?"

"I didn't really—" I began. How was I going to explain this? Why would someone choose to pass for white? "I mean, people said Arizona was really racist, and I thought it would just be . . . easier." As the word came out of my mouth, it sounded terrible.

"Easier?" Ramón said. "Not all of us can make the easy choice. Carajo. Not all of us can just slip out from under racism when we feel like it."

"I didn't—" I tried to explain, but there was no way to explain. I had blown my old cover, and this had to be the new cover. I wasn't a white girl. I was a light Latina girl who chose to pass for white. Ramón liked the white girl. He had stopped feeling ashamed to be with her. But the Latina girl who didn't want to be herself? He was never going to like her. He didn't want her as a girlfriend.

His mouth constricted, like he'd tasted something bitter.

For a wild second, I wanted to tell him everything. But I couldn't betray the cause. Not even for the boy with the sweetest kiss I'd ever tasted. The only kiss. So I took off running for home.

I reached the spot where we'd kissed, but the guys were long gone. And lucky for them. I was spoiling for a fight. I felt so angry and hurt, I would have ripped them limb from limb.

I even thought of trying to find them, but that was ridiculous. My martial arts training taught me never to go looking for a fight. I was a spy. I couldn't jeopardize my cover for something like that. Suddenly, my energy dissipated. The seven steps to the house seemed like a million miles. I trudged up them as if my legs were filled with lead.

When I unlocked the door, Mom was cleaning up in the kitchen.

"How was the festival?" she asked.

"Él ya sabe," I said in a monotone.

"Honey, remember, we said no Spanish,"

"Ramón sabe que somos latinas," I said. "He knows."

"He what?" Mom asked.

"These guys—" I started, and then my face crumpled and the tears began to fall.

"¿Qué pasó?" Mom asked.

I told her the whole terrible story, omitting only the kiss. "I shouldn't have said anything," I said. "I should have figured it out some other way."

"Oh no, honey," she said. "You did the right thing. You did so great. You had to make a split-second decision, and you picked the right thing. It's just . . . sometimes as a spy, you get connected with people you're assigned to, but it . . . it's not real. You knew that, amor. We talked about that."

I nodded through my tears.

"The mission can still go forward," she said. "We

can still talk Kyle and John into going. That's what matters most."

First kiss. First boyfriend for five minutes. I guessed it was just part of being a spy, that you might have your first kiss with someone who didn't even know who you were.

THIRTY

I woke up in the middle of the night and couldn't get back to sleep. I was staring at the blank ceiling, but it became like a movie screen that kept playing the previous scenes of the evening. The drunk guys, Ramón's angry face. It was too much.

I went downstairs and reread one of the Triángulo comics. Anything to keep my mind occupied with something else.

After about twenty minutes of Arantxa saving Manhattan, Mom came downstairs.

"You okay, sweetie?" she asked. *Sweetie?* Even at 3:27 a.m., she was true to her cover.

"I just—" I began. "I mean, I keep thinking about what Ramón said. I know I'm undercover, but it makes me think. I've always just been like, I'm Latina. But if we can so easily convince all these people that we're white . . . does that make us . . . sort of . . . white?"

"No, honey," she said. "White people come from Europe. Our people come from Puerto Rico and Mexico. Even though we have a lot of the colonizers' blood, and the fact is that their genes show in our faces, our lineage is of colonized people. And we're part of the lineage of resistance, too—Indigenous and Black people who have resisted slavery and colonization. And we're still fighting."

I decided to say something I hadn't told her before. "Since I started on this assignment, I've been staring at my face in the mirror," I said. "Like after I come out of the shower and before we press my hair. I've been trying to figure out which parts of me look Puerto Rican, which parts look Mexican, and which parts look white."

"It can be tempting to try to put different parts of you in different boxes," she said. "But we're Latinas. One hundred percent. Just as much as anyone else. Sometimes people who look like us get called white Latinas, referring to the skin-color privilege that we definitely do have. But just because we get mistaken for white, it doesn't mean we're actually white people. Because Latines come in all colors. The problem is that when it's time to show Latine pride—people who are celebrities and role models—a lot of times it's Latines who look like us getting promoted in the community and the media. Not folks who look Indio like Papi. And certainly not anyone who's Black."

I thought about it and realized she was right. Whenever I saw ads for products in our community, nobody ever looked like Papi. And they certainly never looked like Jerrold or Imani.

"The Latine mainstream is always ready to celebrate Africa in our music and our food and our sports heroes," Mami said. "But they're definitely not celebrating Africa in our skin tones. Or in our hair."

I nodded. "But why not?" I asked. "That's stupid."

She smiled bitterly. "It's racism," she said. "I guess in our community you might call it colorism. Because of the life our family leads, you don't get to see it so much. We're spies, fighting for our people. We're isolated from a lot of the mainstream US culture. But racism isn't just part of white culture—it's Latines, too. The prejudice is there. Even in families. Like for me? Growing up in New York City?" Mami shook her head. "My family was racist against Black people. Against Blackness both inside and outside of our family. My abuela totally favored the lighter grandkids."

Whoa. Mami had never told me about this. "And you were one of the lighter grandkids?" I asked.

Mami let out a bark of laughter. "Not with my hair," she said. "I was in the middle. My light cousin with the straight, sandy hair and green eyes was the favorite. I had a darker cousin, with the 'pelo malo' and brown skin. Abuela used to say, 'Thank goodness she's nice and she can cook.'"

My eyes flew wide in shock. "What?" I asked. "She actually said that?"

"Right in front of her," Mami said. "It was terrible."

"Did you say anything?" I asked.

Mami was quiet for a moment. "I know we've taught you to stand up for what you believe," she said. "But you need to understand, it wasn't just that I didn't stand up. There was also some part of me that wasn't clear what I believed."

"You agreed with your grandmother?" I asked, a little horrified.

Mami frowned. "I thought it was a mean thing to say out loud," she said. "But my grandmother believed that being whiter made you better. Everyone in our family and our neighborhood seemed to believe it, too. It was clearly reflected back to me in all forms of the media. I couldn't tell that it was part of the ideology of white supremacy. The lie that whiteness is superior. More intelligent, valuable, beautiful. I thought it was just how the world was. My grandmother's generation had no shame about their racism. My parents were a little different. They didn't say stuff like that out loud. But they would imply things . . . And when other people said racist things, they never stood up."

"Your parents died when you were in high school, right?"

"Yeah," Mami said. "I lived with Abuela after that, but she was too old to take care of an angry teenager like me. I would sneak out all the time. I got into so much trouble."

"And she died before I was born?" I asked.

"Yes," Mami said. "I'm sorry you never got to meet her."

"Even though she was racist?" I asked.

"Yup," Mami said. "That's the messed-up thing about racism in our community. We're a racially mixed people. So the love and the racism are all mixed together."

"But you're different from how she was," I said. "You've committed your life to fighting racism."

She shrugged. "I had to do a lot of work at the Factory," she said. "I thought that I could stand up against racism in the world and not have to look at my own family. And never reveal the ideas that were still in my own head. The racism I had internalized. But I had to stop pretending. I had to look at how racist ideas had hurt me. And how I had participated in hurting people who were darker than I was. I had to uproot all the bias I had."

"How did you unlearn it?" I asked.

She gave a bitter laugh. "I had to start by acknowledging the racist ideas in my head," she said. "And then I had to feel totally mortified that I had them. But people reminded me, it wasn't my fault that I grew up believing those things. And now that I was grown, it was my responsibility to unlearn them. And then I just cried a lot. Remembering how bad it felt to be targeted with colorism. How bad I felt about the times I had targeted other people or stood by and watched them get hurt."

"Yeah," I said. "That does sound hard. Did Papi grow up the same way?"

"He grew up in the western US," she said. "And they were more Indigenous. So they internalized more anti-Indigenous racism. But his family was definitely racist against Black people. We call it anti-Black racism. As Latines, we get targeted with racism from the larger society, but our community is also full of anti-Black racism, targeting Black people outside our community as well as our own Blackness. That's what I grew up with."

She twirled a lock of her hair. "I mean, how do you think I have such good skills in straightening our hair?" she asked. "I did it every day during high school. I'm not talking about flat-ironing it sometimes for a change. I'm talking about never leaving the house with my natural hair. My grandmother just saw it as part of looking 'presentable.' But she really meant looking less Black."

I blinked. I just assumed it was one of the disguise skills Mami learned at the Factory. Like learning martial arts and how to pick locks. But her family had taught her not to accept her hair? Her grandmother had preferred the lighter grandchildren?

I looked up at Mami. I had found her transformation to Barbara Burke so ridiculous. Even almost funny. But now I saw it differently. It was a disguise she had been learning how to wear since long before she ever got to the Factory.

"We've tried to raise you to be proud of your culture, and I hope we've succeeded," she said. "But you can't escape societal biases altogether, and you'll have to grapple with your own light privilege as you grow up, too. Just know that we'll be here to talk with you about it whenever you want."

She squeezed my shoulder. "Come on, dear," she said, slipping effortlessly back into her Barbara Burke cover—*dear*. "Let's go back to bed."

I nodded. With every step up the stairs, I felt exhausted. Like the weight of everything my mother had said was pressing down on me. I dragged myself into the bedroom and could barely make the last few steps to the bed.

When I woke up, I found I had crashed out on top of the covers. Slowly, the night before came back to me. The racist guys. Ramón. All that my mom had said. But there were no emotions attached to it. I felt numb, spent.

I rolled over to look at my phone, and there was a text from Kyle:

> Ramón says he's not going to ComxCon because you're
> Latina and you didn't say it before? Which makes no sense
> because he's always saying he wants to hang with more
> Latinxs. I don't get it. Like move on, dude. But if he's going
> to let a little thing like this get in the way of the trip and
> ruin your friendship, it's his loss. Me and my dad are
> still in.

I felt for Ramón. The guy closest to him totally didn't get anything about the complexity of race. And there was that word: "friendship." Ramón still hadn't said anything to Kyle.

Maybe he would have told him if I hadn't ruined everything. My eyes went to the drawing of me that Ramón had done on the napkin in the pizza place. Me looking white. Then the numbness collapsed and I felt something. I started crying again.

THIRTY-ONE

Dear teenagers of the world, if you are going to have a painful breakup, do it during exam week or spring cleaning or some other busy time of year. Do not do it during a week when you have nothing, *literally nothing*, to do.

Every day was excruciating. I didn't have school (although that would have been worse because I would have had to see Ramón). I didn't have a lot to do for work. We were just waiting for ComxCon.

On the eve of our trip to San Diego, Jerrold updated me with all the details of the operation. He asked if I had any questions.

I had several about the logistics. And then I asked

the big one I had been wondering about the entire assignment.

"I still don't understand why you picked me," I said. "For this operation."

"You were the right age, the right appearance," Jerrold said. "Your mom was worried, but I've been handling your family for years. I thought you were ready."

"But the race thing," I said.

Jerrold steepled his fingers under his chin. I could see a lecture coming. "When it comes to racists, we can't send operatives who are obviously people of color," he said.

"And Mom said you don't send white people because they underestimate the danger," I said.

"That's right," he said. "They just don't have the same natural danger radar and vigilance that teens of color have."

"But I'm just a hairstyle away from looking like a white girl next door," I said. "How can I have that natural vigilance?"

"You didn't grow up in a vacuum," he said. "Your mother moved to New York from Puerto Rico. A native speaker of Spanish who had to do years of training to unlearn her accent so she could be a more effective spy. You grew up as a child of Spanish speakers. Your dad and brother are obviously of color. Just because you can pass for white doesn't mean your whole family can.

For the first decade of your life, you were obviously of color because you moved in the world in the context of your family. When people gave them dirty looks for speaking Spanish, you also felt it. When people talked about building a huge wall on the Mexico border, that was about keeping your father's people out. When Hurricane María hit Puerto Rico, it was your mother's people who were left to die. Chances are that in some situations you got favored because of your color. But you didn't escape racism. Racism doesn't happen only to individuals. It also happens to families and communities."

"I never thought about it that way," I said.

"People talk about impostor syndrome for people of color," Jerrold said. "They use it to describe how we feel when we're in college or successful in our fields. We feel anxious, like we don't belong and we're going to be found out, and this emotional experience can be crippling. But I can't really imagine what it would feel like if Black people didn't always recognize me, didn't always acknowledge me. I imagine that would be challenging in a different way."

"I don't know, Jerrold," I said. "People of color have real issues, life-and-death dangers beyond feeling invisible to our people. Like, I'm not someone who's likely to get shot by police."

He nodded. "That's true," he said. "There's a whole body of research that shows discrepancies between lighter- and darker-skinned people of color. Disparities in income, occupations, education levels, health outcomes . . . you name it. We have the data on color. We can map it, graph it, and a lot of outcomes get worse for darker people. And at the same time, there's more than one experience of racism. If we defined racism only as having your village razed and getting forcibly sent to an abusive boarding school, or only being barred from entering the country, we'd ignore slavery and anti-Black racism. But if we define racism as only what happens when people exploit your labor, we'd ignore other aspects of Native genocide. If we only define it as mistreatment based on perceived difference in skin color or appearance, we'd ignore a lot of important facets of racism: appropriation, exploitation, exotification, so many issues. And there's a light-skinned experience of racism that has different damage."

"How does it damage me to have this kind of privilege?" I asked.

"White supremacy damages everyone," he said. "It's a system based on lies, violence, and exploitation. Part of the systemic damage is when people of color grow up thinking white people are better, and using that logic to think that lighter people are better. The damage is having a distorted perspective and relationship with your own people. It's a brutal harm. Especially if people disconnect from their communities and then feel like that disconnection equals success. Just because someone's life looks prosperous and shiny on the outside doesn't mean that it looks good on the inside."

I knew this was true from social media. People can appear really happy and successful, but actually feel awful.

"And it can go beyond disconnection," Jerrold went on. "Sometimes lighter folks turn on their own people. White supremacy has always rewarded that kind of backstabbing as part of a strategy of divide and conquer. But that backstabbing behavior is ultimately based on self-hatred and shame about their roots, their families, and themselves. Internalized racism can be unlearned. Your mom did it. And if you truly feel love for all your people of color, and you stand up against every form of racism, you can be fully connected to your community, regardless of the skin and hair and features that you happen to have."

"I hope so," I said.

"I'm going to give you a couple hours to meditate on these questions, because I know they're looming large for you right now," he said. "But by tonight, I need your A game. The most important thing is stopping the terrorist."

THIRTY-TWO

From the moment we arrived in the San Diego airport, there was a sense of anticipation. So many people with their hair dyed bright colors. People who seemed to regard long dark capes as everyday wear. Oddly long bags and packages being picked up off the carousels at baggage claim. A few people fully in costume already, even though we had arrived a day early.

We had spent the plane ride studying the updates to the ComxCon schedule and getting acclimated to the convention app on our phones. The first day, there was a huge session called "Triángulo: How Latin America Took Over Comics and Cards This Year." We decided that was the kind of thing that would attract Dave—a totally articulated threat to white supremacy.

A Factory car picked us up and drove us straight

to the hotel. Imani and I studied the blueprints of the convention center and all the briefing materials until Mom insisted we go to bed.

I finally fell asleep around two in the morning. And then I was up again a little before six. I wandered into the suite's living room and read a Triángulo graphic novel. The next thing I knew, Mom was waking me up.

I was lying on the couch, and she took the graphic novel off my chest.

"Despiértate, amor," she said.

Not Mom. Mami. I reached up and hugged her close. She squeezed back and then kissed my temple as she let go.

She looked at me and smoothed my hair back from my forehead. "Come on," she said. "Imani's already up. You need to hurry and put on the costumes Jerrold sent over."

Initially, Mom worried that wearing costumes was a bad idea, because it would increase fans interacting with us: taking pictures, commenting, and distracting us from our work. But Jerrold thought it would help us to blend in, and there would be so many people in costume there that we wouldn't be distracted. Which turned out to be true. When we got there, seven Arantxas walked by in the first five minutes.

To cosplay Arantxa, I needed curly hair. There were cheap shiny brown wigs for sale online, but my natural hair was the perfect texture—maybe just a shade light for her.

I showered and wore my hair loose. I pulled on the brown unitard, the gold boots and gloves, and the gold sash tied at the hip. It kept slipping, so I triple-knotted it. I felt uncomfortable with the way the shape of my body showed beneath the unitard. I never wore tight clothing unless I was going swimming. The brown mask made me feel a bit more anonymous, but still exposed. At least the brown cape covered my butt.

I went into the suite's living room to look for Imani. Mom had gone out to meet with Jerrold before we all headed over to the Con.

Imani came out of the other bedroom in her Olumide costume. It was even flashier than mine. The unitard and mask were dark blue, but the boots, trim, and cape were covered in turquoise sequins. Her body was way curvier than mine, but she seemed totally comfortable in the clingy outfit. She had taken out her braids and combed her hair into a big Afro. She looked amazing.

We heard the hotel lock beep and click open.

"Look at you two!" Mom said as she came in. She set down her briefcase on the couch and pulled out her phone. "Girls, can I take a quick picture before we hit the road?"

I rolled my eyes. Imani shrugged.

"Pleeeease?" Mom asked. "Just let me text this to

the fam. Both of the families. I promise to be a good spy for the rest of the day."

"Come on," Imani sang, and put an arm around me. I resigned myself and posed reluctantly.

"Say 'Stop that terrorist!'" Mom said, and snapped the picture.

Our hotel was close to ComxCon, and traffic was backed up. There was a palpable energy around us. People were excited. I wished that the knot in my stomach and my increased heartbeat were caused by wondering how I'd do in the costume contest or if I'd get an autograph from my favorite author, instead of wondering if we'd catch a man hell-bent on race war who wanted to kill huge numbers of people of color.

We weren't totally sure what weapon he was going to use, but we had gas masks in our backpacks.

When we finally got close to the Con, I panicked. There. Were. So. Many. People. It's one thing to hear that over 130,000 people come to something. It's another thing to be there and see the crowds.

It was an explosion of color, sparkle, costumes, bright wigs, jumbotrons, posters, and technology. Half the people were looking at devices with the ComxCon app. Others were taking selfies or pictures of their friends. The cosplay was crazy, with about a third of the folks in costume. There was a weapons check, where they verified that people's swords, guns, and daggers weren't real. They gave a little sticker to prove that you'd been screened. I saw a couple of signs that said, "Cosplay is not consent," which was great, since some girls were in super-skimpy costumes, and some guys will take advantage of that to be like, *But if she didn't want me grabbing her, why was she wearing that?* Come on, dude. In this day and age, you've heard of sexual harassment, right?

We met up with Kyle and John at my mom's "booth." In reality, she was holding down the HQ for the Factory, right between virtual reality systems and custom-designed cosplay weapons.

Kyle lit up when he saw our costumes. He jumped up and said a few Naturalezo lines. John Summer smiled politely at our costumes, too, but I noticed that he really beamed when he looked at his son.

There was so much energy on the floor that our mission felt surreal. Up until now, I hadn't really understood the cosplay thing. But with my Arantxa costume on, I sort of felt like a kid at Halloween again. I got so excited that I had to remind myself I was going to the Con to work, not play.

We spent some time walking around the floor with Kyle and John and keeping a sharp eye out for the terrorist. There were so many people that it was like searching for a needle in a haystack, but at least looking for a tall blond guy wearing a gas mask narrowed it down.

"Dad, can we go to the Star Battle installation?" Kyle asked.

"Sure, Kyle," John said. "Whatever you want."

"You guys coming?" Kyle asked.

Imani and I looked at each other and shrugged. We needed to separate from Kyle and John so that we could check in with the team, while still being able to find them to confirm an ID if we spotted Dave.

"Not really our thing," Imani said. "But it's next to the space burgers. Let's meet there for lunch afterward."

"Sounds great," I said. "You guys like burgers?"

Kyle and his dad looked at each other.

"Yeah," Kyle said. "Dad?"

"Sure," he said awkwardly. "I like a good burger."

Kyle looked relieved.

It must be weird to be hanging out with your dad and not knowing basic things about him.

We said our goodbyes and peeled off from Kyle and John. Once they were out of sight, we put in earbuds and hunched over Imani's phone in the corner for a videoconference with Mom and Jerrold.

"Head of security is detaining a guy with a real gas mask and a suitcase he refuses to open," Jerrold said. "We sent over the sketches, and he says the guy fits the description."

"What does your FBI guy say?" Mom asked.

Jerrold's mouth tightened. "The FBI sent him on another assignment at the last minute," he said.

"What?" Mom said. "They couldn't even spare *one* agent? Not even after we sent them all that intel?"

"I know, Bárbara," Jerrold said. "They're using our sting-gone-wrong as an excuse to deprioritize something that was never a priority. We can't let it throw us."

Mom let out her breath in a huff. "So it's up to our team."

"We can do this," Jerrold said. "Hector, you're closest to the front gate. Can you go see if you can get a look at the guy?"

"I'm on it," Hector's voice crackled through the earbuds.

"I'll try to get into security," Jerrold said. "But without my FBI contact, I'm having to improvise. I think the next step is to get John over here to ID the guy."

"Okay," I said. "We'll handle that."

Kyle and John met us at the food stand, and we all had space burgers. Which were basically just burgers with a little Saturn planet toasted onto the bun.

Just as we finished, I pressed the button that made my phone do a text chime. Then I pretended to read an incoming text.

"John," I said. "You'll never believe it. In a freak coincidence, my mom thinks she might have found the identity thief!"

"She what?" John asked.

We hurried him down the hall.

"I know," Imani said. "Is that, like, one-in-a-billion odds?"

"ComxCon is a place where magical things can happen," I said.

We passed a session called "Triángulo for LGBTQ+ Teens." It was full and there was overflow into the hallway. Everything bottlenecked, and it took a while to get through. Near the door stood a cute boy dressed as Arantxa. He smiled at Kyle.

Kyle literally looked around like, *Who? Me?*

The boy smiled even brighter.

"Hey," Imani said. "No need for you to come with us, Kyle. You should check out this session. For the whole team."

"Uh, yeah," Kyle said. "Is that okay, Dad?"

John was frowning deeply, clearly focused on facing off with the man he had known as Dave. "Sure," he told Kyle absently.

"Take good notes," I said to Kyle. "Come on, John."

I took John by the arm and pulled him toward security.

When we got to the security room, Jerrold was standing there in a thick-framed pair of glasses I'd never seen before. Instead of his usual classic three-piece suit, he had on a light brown jacket with jeans. No tie. And instead of his usual fancy dress shoes, he had on sneakers. Next to him stood a young Latina woman.

I was surprised that Mom wasn't there. I texted to find out where she was.

"John Summer?" Jerrold asked.

"Yeah," he said in an agitated tone. "The girls told me—"

Jerrold cut him off and lowered his voice. "There's a man they have in custody here, and I think he might be your identity thief," he said. "I work with Barbara in cybersecurity, and I think they caught the guy here up to some kind of shenanigans."

Shenanigans? I almost laughed out loud. Unless he was undercover, Jerrold would never say "shenanigans."

"Let me see the guy," John said. "I'd know him in a heartbeat."

"That's just it," Jerrold said. "I don't really have any jurisdiction here. Security is pretty tight. They're not letting me back to look at him. But at some point, they've got to bring him out."

"Oh, I'll wait," John said. He was fully heated now, ready for a fight.

"I'll go see if I can find out anything," the young Latina woman said, and disappeared down the hall.

There was a bench against the wall where Jerrold and John sat down.

I expected Mom to get right back to me, but she hadn't.

"Okay, girls," John said. "Tell Barbara I can't thank her enough."

"Sure," I said.

"Well, what are you waiting for?" he asked. "You all need to get back to enjoying yourselves."

Imani and I glanced at each other. That wasn't the plan—we needed to be there to confirm we had the right guy.

"Are you kidding me?" Imani said. "We're like junior detectives. We wanna see this guy."

"Yeah," I chimed in. "A real identity thief. My mom has been talking about these guys all my life."

We stood around awkwardly for ten minutes, trying to maintain an expectant look on our faces.

Stakeouts were the most boring part of spy work. You had to wait while nothing was happening, but you couldn't stop paying attention.

Imani texted me in the first five minutes and established that we would take turns being alert so that the other one could zone out on her phone.

But then there was an announcement that the big Triángulo session was about to start in the main auditorium.

"Go ahead, girls," John Summer said. "I'll see you afterward."

Imani and I looked at each other.

"We were gonna wait here," Imani said.

"Yeah," I added. "To see the real criminal."

"No way," John said. "Kyle talked about what a big deal this is for Triángulo fans. Historic. International. A sneak preview of the movie no one has seen yet. I can't believe that two teen Triángulo fans would miss that to see some loser who stole my driver's license a long time ago. Unless there's some other reason you want to stay?"

We looked at Jerrold. "For all we know," he said, "this guy may not even come out during that time. You girls could check back afterward."

"Okay," I said, trying not to look too enthusiastic.

Imani took my hand, and we slipped into the crowd drifting toward the main auditorium.

We walked down a long fluorescent-lit corridor toward where we had left Kyle. On our way, we saw two cosplayers—both dressed as Black Panther—who crossed paths. They gave each other the "Wakanda forever!" greeting and then hugged. Imani pulled out her phone and snapped their photo. One of them gave her a flyer to AfroComicCon in Oakland.

Meanwhile, my phone rang with my mother's ringtone.

"Mom," I said. "Where have you been? Is there an update?"

Imani and I huddled in a corner with the phone on speaker but low.

"Sorry I couldn't respond," Mom said. "There have been two big developments. First off, security confirmed that the guy in custody has an actual weapon. He's saying it's not his, that it belongs to his brother. He insists that the brother is coming to explain it all. Yeah, good luck with that. Explaining a chemical weapon. I'm sure his 'brother' is long gone by now."

A huge weight lifted off my chest. Imani looked at me, eyes wide. I gave her a big thumbs-up sign.

"But here's the biggest thing," Mom said. "Our techs were able to hack into the security footage, and when they sent it to Jerrold, John identified the guy he knew as Dave."

"For real?" I asked.

"Yes," she said. "He was positive. Now we're just waiting to make double sure with the in-person ID. But at this point, it's just a formality."

"Does that mean we're just two teenagers at a ComxCon?" Imani asked.

"Absolutely," Mom said. "You're giving the organization your teen years. You just furnished the critical piece of information to stop a terrorist attack. You can have fun for half a day."

"Yes!" Imani said. "So we can really enjoy the big Triángulo session."

But as we made our way to the main hall, I kept noticing all the BaguaNi cosplayers that weren't Ramón. And I couldn't stop myself from scanning faces, looking at tall men. I couldn't shake the feeling that there was still danger.

THIRTY-THREE

We got to the main stage twenty minutes later—it took forever just to get from one place to another, since the hallway was mobbed as people filed in for the Triángulo session. Imani went to save us seats while I texted Kyle to find out where he was.

"I'm at the door to the main-stage auditorium."

"Which one?" I wrote back. "There are like twenty doors."

He sent a laughing emoji. We decided he would walk clockwise and I'd walk counterclockwise until we found each other.

Kyle had a surprise. Next to him was the cute guy from the teen Triángulo session.

"This is Bradley," Kyle said with a shy smile.

"Great to meet you," I said, gesturing at his costume. "Twinsies!"

We grinned at each other. I texted Imani to save a fourth seat.

"Is John back?" she texted.

"No," I wrote back. "Kyle has a DATE!"

She sent a shock face emoji and a heart eyes emoji. I kept a poker face as we made our way to the seats.

We were sitting on the side aisle, toward the front.

"Wow," I said. "How'd you get such good seats?'

"People in Triángulo costumes get priority seating," Bradley said.

"I like this session already," I said.

The first panelist introduced was Angelica Dominguez, the Dominican woman from New York who had started the comic book. She had a wild auburn Afro and a bright smile with a gap between her teeth. There was also the man from Brazil who had turned it into a card game. He was older, like Jerrold's age, with a bright African-print tunic. Finally, there was a petite Nicaraguan American woman with blue hair, who was making the film version.

They showed a trailer from the upcoming Triángulo movie. We all watched Arantxa, Olumide, and BaguaNi get shot through a time-travel portal, back to the seventeenth century. Because they're in another era, they find themselves stripped of their powers, running along a beach on Caguama Island, looking for the Maroon colony. They come face-to-face with the original Naturalezo, the young enslaver, before he was fully corrupted by the magic that was never meant for him. A voiceover says, "Can they fix the future by changing the past?"

After the trailer, everyone was cheering, and the whole room was super excited. I had been pretty high-energy all day, but at that moment, with everyone cheering, I felt my heart sink a little. I really wished that Ramón could have been there.

When the panelists started the discussion, I closed my eyes and basked in the Spanish and Portuguese accents and the sprinkling of Spanglish, especially by Angelica Dominguez, whose New York accent sounded so much like my mom when she wasn't undercover.

"A lot of people don't like us," she was saying. "They're afraid of us. Afraid of what we represent. We're the majority in the world, and by far the majority in this hemisphere. We're taking our rightful place. In comics. In games. In movies. In the world. And no one can stop us."

The room erupted in cheering.

I squeezed Imani's hand and started crying. Someone *had* tried to stop them. But we had worked hard—and our organization had worked hard—to make sure he wouldn't be successful. The institutions that were supposed to help us had failed. The police. The FBI. They were too soft on racism to make it a priority. Our people had stepped up and eliminated the threat. I cried harder, which was why I didn't hear Imani right away when she started saying, "Go!"

I looked at her, disoriented, wiping my eyes.

"They're calling the people in costume to the stage!" she said. "Come on!"

I was on the aisle, and I stood up quickly, rushing into the line. Imani was right behind me. I dried my eyes with my cape, and we pressed forward.

"Isn't Bradley coming?" I asked.

"He wanted to stay with Kyle," Imani said, and we high-fived.

The line of people in costume moved forward. The area backstage was filling up.

"Okay," said Angelica with a laugh. "We had no idea there would be so many of you. We can fit a few more."

A security guard waved Imani in. "She's the last one." She pulled a retractable gate closed in front of me.

"Can you take my friend instead?" Imani asked.

"Sure," said the guard. "Just one. You decide."

"No way," I said.

"Girl," Imani began. "It's your first—um—ComxCon where you were—um—the focus," she said. "Not just coming along with your parents, but you being the main . . . cosplayer. You need to celebrate."

Imani opened the gate and stepped out, putting a hand at the small of my back to gently guide me backstage. The guard pulled the divider shut.

I was still weepy. I guessed it was all the pent-up emotions and tensions of the past month.

"For my first . . . ComxCon," I said. "I was so lucky to have you by my side. I never could have . . . made such an amazing costume and had such a good . . . experience without you. You're the best . . . Triángulo player a girl could hope to have when going up against . . . Naturalezo."

"I've been to ComxCon before . . . but it's so different when you're with somebody else," she said. "Somebody on my team. Some of the . . . sessions can be really hard, and it's such a relief to have somebody to go with. Not to mention, somebody to be with . . . between sessions. You know? I've been to ComxCon with my parents before, but it's not like having somebody my own age. I feel so lucky."

"I'm gonna miss you so much after . . . ComxCon is over," I said.

Imani teared up and pressed her lips tight. "Same here," she said.

The security guard sent the rest of the line to their seats.

"Wow," a girl in costume nearby said to her friend. "I like a good Con, but some people are really extra."

• • •

From our area in the wings, the view was amazing. A huge room filled with fans, many of them in costume. These were my people. Mi gente.

I looked across the stage, and there were so many of us representing for Triángulo. Teens, adults, Latine folks, Black folks, white folks, everybody. I was one of a multitude of Arantxas. But there were Olumides and BaguaNis, too. And even a few Naturalezos.

The villains ranged in costume. There were some who dressed as Naturalezo when he was at his full power—muscle suit with oversize calves and distorted chest. Then there were those who dressed as the villain when he first discovered his power and had the body of a regular slender young man. These guys were really serious about their villains. They were dressed in costumes from obscure issues, like his steampunk outfit, his Zorro look, and the toxic sky showdown episode where he had on the gas mask. That was the version of the villain Imani and I had been on the lookout for.

One of the Naturalezos was tall and Black. Really? I couldn't imagine why someone Black would dress up as a white descendant of enslavers, but maybe he was part of a Black crew that was doing all the costumes?

In my hip pocket, my silenced phone vibrated. I had to reach under the costume to get to the side pocket on my leggings. It was super awkward.

I finally pulled my phone out, and on the lock screen

was a text from Mom in all caps: "WRONG MAN IN CUSTODY! TERRORIST STILL AT LARGE!"

I felt a cold panic sweep over my entire body.

Angelica Dominguez was onstage saying something, but suddenly I couldn't hear anything for the rushing in my ears. It took me a moment to get hold of myself, for rational thought to return.

I shuddered hard and recalled my surroundings.

Still at large? I looked around me, and there were at least ten Naturalezos. A half dozen of them were in the gas mask costume.

I looked on the stage and saw the panel of creators. All brown. Mostly female.

This was the main-stage Triángulo event. Thousands of people in the audience. This would be the target. What had Angelica Dominguez said? "We're the majority in the world . . . We're taking our rightful place . . . No one can stop us."

But the terrorist was determined to try. Thanks to his costume, he would have been invited onstage. There were only maybe seventy-five cosplayers. But there were way too many Naturalezos. Which one was he? They kept moving around!

I began a process of elimination. Far off to my right, there was one, but he was too short. Not only could I eliminate the Black one, but another one ahead of me had dark curly hair and tawny skin. Also, whoever I was looking for would likely be getting ready to go onstage.

I pressed forward toward the line where the costumed crowd ended and the open stage began.

There was one tall Naturalezo in the front. Could that be him? Wait! There were two others. One was just a few paces back from the front. The other was far to my right, away from the audience. They were all tall, all apparently white, with various lengths of straightish, sandy-brown hair. I couldn't see any of their faces in the gas masks. How could I possibly identify him? How would I possibly know?

I moved around in the crowd till I was at the center point between the three of them, so if one of them made a move, I could be as close as possible. Fortunately, they were tall enough that I could keep track of them in the crowd.

I turned around and looked for security but saw only the crush of fans in Triángulo costumes.

Why hadn't I trusted my gut? I had left my backpack with the gas mask at the booth. I thought the threat was over. Now there was a terrorist up front—possibly armed with a chemical weapon—and nobody on the stage knew but me.

THIRTY-FOUR

My heart pounded in my throat as I stood and waited. Just a moment ago, the crush of people had seemed exhilarating. Now it seemed claustrophobic and dangerous.

The second Naturalezo seemed to be on the move, heading toward the front of the cosplayers, toward the open stage. Was he going to attack? Or just trying to get a better view?

I kept my eye on the back of his head, the plastic straps of the gas mask crisscrossing through his hair. As I headed his way, I kept turning around to keep tabs on the other two Naturalezos. I hadn't made a definitive identification. I couldn't zero in on one until I knew for sure. When I reached the one up front, I swallowed hard against the heartbeat in my throat.

But then I saw the other Naturalezo—the one

who was already at the front—move forward as well. He stood at the edge of the costumed masses with his hands at his sides. His stance looked more tense than the other one. He balled his fists and then released them. He did it a few times. Was he tense? Was he angry? Was he just nervous standing onstage in front of so many people? And then he tapped on the sides of his thighs. My breath stopped for a minute. It was the same gesture I had seen when I was lying beneath an SUV in the parking lot outside Heather McClelland's apartment.

I surged forward in the crowd, not sure what I would even do. All I had was my knife and the belt to my costume, which was made of a really strong textile. I tried to pull it off, but I had knotted it too tightly. It was taking too long to untie. Instead, I pulled out the knife and took off my mask, which was made of the same strong textile.

I slipped into a small gap in the crowd on the left of the terrorist. I looked up at him and grinned. "Wow," I said. "Amazing costume. Makes me almost ready to be a bad guy." I smiled, like I was totally fangirling.

The gas mask obscured the lower half of his face, but I looked up through plastic lenses into eyes that chilled me. They definitely belonged to the man who had been banging on Heather McClelland's door.

I kept my face warm and open as I surveyed his whole costume.

"Whoa," I added. "Those gloves are amazing. They're handmade, right? Can I see?"

I lifted both his hands up and quickly tightened my Arantxa mask over them. I used my knife to slice the straps holding the tank on his back. I grabbed the tank—it was heavier than I thought. I tried to run deeper into the backstage, but it was too crowded. The only path away from him was onto the stage. I ran out, putting the panelists between me and him.

The lights were hot and harsh against my bare shoulders and arms.

The moment I hit the stage, the crowd erupted into applause. When Naturalezo came running after me, they booed heartily.

I set down the tank and leaped on him, using a few martial arts moves to pin him down. The crowd erupted in wild cheers.

"Get off me!" he said. "This isn't a comic book."

Behind me, I could hear the security guard talking to the comic book creator. "I'm so sorry," she said. "We'll get them off the stage."

"No," Angelica Dominguez said. "This is great. It's all about the fans. Let them play the scene."

"I know who you are," I said. "And you won't be detonating any chemical weapons today."

"You think I can't detonate it remotely?" he asked.

My chest burned with horror. I had underestimated him.

I looked out into the audience to find Imani, but she wasn't in her seat. Just Kyle and Bradley, grinning at me.

No, no, NO!

A sea of camera phones were up in the audience.

"Turn up the mics," someone from the audience yelled. "We can't hear what she's saying."

I leaned down and ripped off his mask.

"You can't detonate without killing yourself as well," I said.

"You think I wouldn't die for the cause?" he asked. "You're a disgrace to the white race!"

"I'm Latina, you pendejo!" I yelled. I was shocked to hear my voice booming through the sound system.

Where did he have the detonator? In his coat? In one of his gloves? A pants pocket?

When I reached into his coat pocket, he twisted out of my hold and stood up.

I leaped to my feet. We circled each other, him looking for an opening to go for the detonator, and me waiting for him to make his move so I could strike while his hands were busy.

Finally, he reached for it, in his pants pocket. I jumped up and tackled him again, but he managed to get something into his hands. He skidded across the stage and held up the detonator.

"Stay back!" he said.

I had no choice but to back off.

I had failed. I prayed he was bluffing.

He stepped up to the microphone and savored the moment, looking from one end of the room to the other, taking in all the faces.

I was standing a little in front of him, looking back at all the costumed people at the rear of the stage.

"This is for the white—"

Which is when Imani broke through the cosplayers and zapped him with the security guard's Taser.

The terrorist fell, and the crowd went berserk.

Imani held the Taser up for me to take. I stepped over to grab it, while she retreated back into the costumed crowd. Then suddenly, the young Latina "security guard" who had been with Jerrold walked up to the mic. "Let's get this creep Naturalezo out of here, shall we?"

The crowd was cheering wildly.

She took the remote out of his hand, and I gave her the Taser. Two other guards came up and dragged the terrorist off the stage. I didn't know if they were real security or with our operation. The guard I recognized walked over to the tank I'd sliced off his back. I met her eyes, and she carried it offstage.

Angelica Dominguez came over to me and held my hand up in the air. "Arantxa, everybody! Let's hear it for fierce Latinas!"

The room went crazy.

But then a man in a suit came up to the moderator and spoke to Angelica. Her eyes widened, and she turned back to the mic.

"Oh-kay . . . so don't panic, everybody," she said. "But it turns out that the man onstage wasn't a cosplayer. He was actually armed and dangerous. Apparently, the FBI was about to apprehend him, but this young lady got to him first."

There was a buzz of energy, and all eyes turned to me.

I tried to back off the stage, but Angelica put an arm around my shoulder and asked me, "Did you know he was armed?"

"I—" What was I supposed to say? I wasn't supposed to blow my cover, despite the fact that I had been videotaped on the ComxCon main stage, unmasked, fighting a terrorist.

"I was—" I looked for where Imani had been sitting in the audience to see if she was back. Instead, Jerrold sat there, next to Kyle and Bradley. Jerrold shook his head slightly and frowned.

"No," I said. "I had seen him backstage and everybody else was so enthusiastic and joyful, and he was just—I don't know . . . he seemed to be acting . . . really suspiciously. Like kind of hostile. I noticed his weapon didn't have a clearance sticker. I was like, why would a guy be standing backstage scowling with an unauthorized weapon, you know? And then when he stepped onto the stage, I was worried. So I just—I just did what I had to do."

I looked down at Jerrold. He was nodding.

The next thing I knew, the press was surrounding me. Out of nowhere, an FBI guy came forward and elbowed his way in front of me.

"No more questions, please," he said. "This young lady obviously is just a concerned citizen. If you'll follow me, the Bureau will be holding a press conference in the media lounge, at which time, we will be able to give full details about our ongoing work to end terrorism and answer all of your questions."

And then he left me on the stage. The press trailed after him, but Angelica kept her arm around me and put a mic in front of my face.

"What's your name?"

I looked at Jerrold, and he nodded and shrugged. We both knew that my cover was blown. There was no point in trying to protect my identity anymore. "Andréa," I said, finally pronouncing my name correctly in Spanish.

"Where are you from?" the artist asked.

"Los Angeles," I said.

"And you're Latina?" she asked.

"Yeah," I said. "My mom is Puerto Rican and my dad's Mexican."

"That's why I wrote the comic book in the first place,"

Angelica said. "To inspire young Latinxs to find ways to be heroic in their everyday lives. I never expected something like this." She held my hand up, like I'd just won a boxing match or something. "¡Gracias, Andréa!"

The crowd was on their feet.

The moderator closed the session, and I tried to get off the stage, but I was mobbed by fans. Most of them wanted to take selfies with me, but some wanted autographs. I obliged all of them and was exhausted by the time our security guard came up to get me.

"What the heck happened?" I asked. "Were there two terrorists?"

She shook her head. "No," she said. "The guy's brother did eventually show up. It wasn't a weapon, really. It was a confetti shooter. The brother was secretly proposing to his girlfriend."

"Ugh," I said. "Are you serious?"

"Yeah," she said. "Apparently, he took off all the confetti markings so it wouldn't spoil the surprise." She showed me a picture of it. It really did look like a serious weapon. "It's just bad luck that he looked enough like the real terrorist for John Summer to be confused. I think he wanted to catch the identity thief so badly that he convinced himself that it was him."

"Where is everybody?" I asked her.

"The team is back at the hotel," she said.

"Am I the only one who's blown?" I asked.

"I think so," she said. "Pictures of Imani might end

up on social media, but she had on the mask. Everyone else is all clear."

"Kyle and John?" I asked.

"Kyle is in the lounge impressing Bradley and people on social media with the fact that he's one of your best friends," she said, laughing.

"If he only knew he was the whole reason I got pulled into this," I said.

"But he never will," she said, and we ducked into a back hallway for staff only.

I sat around with Imani, Kyle, Bradley, Mom, and John in the hotel, watching the news on various channels. I was back to pretending to be a normal fourteen-year-old. A "spunky Latina teenager" and "a cosplayer turned real-life hero" and "a ComxCon true crime crusader."

We sat around and laughed and ate popcorn and cheered.

"I knew Dave was an identity thief," John said. "But I had no idea he was so dangerous."

We also watched a prerelease cut of the Triángulo movie, since the director had given me a passcode to watch it online. As I had expected, it was amazing!

By the time it was over, it was nearly midnight.

"Okay, folks," Mom said. "It's time to get these girls to bed."

"A whole other day of ComxCon tomorrow!" Kyle said.

"I don't think we're gonna make it," Mom said. "ANN-drea's stepdad saw us on TV and is . . . well, he wants us to come back to LA, to try being a family again. ANN-drea said she was willing to give it a go, too, right, honey?"

"Right," I said. I was impressed. I had wondered how she was going to explain our leaving Arizona. But she stayed true to her Barbara Burke cover, right down to mispronouncing my name.

"Like our family," Kyle said.

"We'll see," Mom said.

Kyle jumped up and hugged me. "Stay in touch," he said.

"I will," I said. And now that I was blown, I could.

As he hugged me, he whispered in my ear, "Wish me luck tonight. I'm hoping for my first kiss . . ."

"Good luck," I said.

The three of them walked to the hotel room door. "I'll meet you in the room, Dad," Kyle said. "I'm gonna walk Bradley to his rideshare downstairs."

The thought of first kisses made me wistful but not regretful. What happened with Ramón was minor compared to fulfilling my mission, even if my cover was blown in the process.

"I wonder what excuse they'll come up with to get me out of Arizona," Imani said after they closed the door.

"Maybe they'll send you to boarding school," I said.

"Or maybe I've been wilding out too much, and they're sending me down south to be with my grandmother in Georgia."

"You have a grandmother in Georgia?" I asked.

"There's one in my cover story," she said.

"I've got it!" I said. "Maybe you didn't have permission to go on this trip at all. And your mom saw me on social media and realized you weren't really sleeping over at my house!"

"Oh, that's good," she said. "I'll suggest that to Jerrold."

THIRTY-FIVE

Mom and I were both tired when we landed in the Phoenix airport, but I was relieved, too. All we had to do now was clear out our base of operations, and we could go home. Mom went to the baggage claim to get our luggage while I went to stand in line for a cab.

The minute I stepped out of the airport, a grinning blond woman came rushing toward me with a microphone in her hand, wielding it almost like a weapon.

"Hello, ANN-drea. I'm Lydia Charles from Channel Four News, and we're live at the Phoenix airport. How are you feeling after your victorious takedown of a suspected terrorist?"

"I . . . uh . . ."

And then, as if I weren't far enough off balance, Mandy ran up and hugged me.

"ANN-drea!" she yelled. "I'm so glad you're okay!" Then she turned to the camera. "I was the first student at Calvin Coolidge High who met ANN-drea and showed her around. Her first school friend."

"That's not—" I began, but she cut me off.

"ANN-drea, I had no idea you were a Latina."

"Yeah, well, that was because I was—because so many of the things you and your friends said were really raci—"

But Lydia had already begun to pull the mic away from me. "And there you have it," the newscaster said. "A joyful reunion for ANN-drea Burke and one of her high school friends here at the Phoenix airport. I'm Lydia Charles reporting live. Back to you, Stan."

I looked from Lydia to Mandy, and I saw the resemblance. This was her mom who worked in TV news.

"Unbelievable" was all I could say, and I walked past them to the taxi stand.

Later, I would look at the clip on the internet, and you really couldn't hear me call her racist, at all. Not even if you turned the volume all the way up.

But someone did make a great mash-up meme that circulated around on social media. The first clip was of Mandy looking clueless and saying, "I had no idea you were a Latina," and they edited it together with the clip from ComxCon of me saying, "I'm Latina, you pendejo." But they tweaked the audio so I sounded like I was saying "pendeja." That made me feel a little better.

Back at the house, Mom and I packed up. It didn't take long.

I didn't have to flat-iron my hair anymore. I just pulled it back in a braid.

I returned all the big-eyed animals to their original places.

We were getting picked up at 4 p.m. to go back to the airport. At three, we heard a knock.

"They're early," I said, and walked to the door.

"Or maybe it's the fake great-aunt, come to see us off," Mom said. She walked into the bedroom to get her suitcase.

I opened the door to find Ramón.

"Hi," I said, startled.

"Hi," he said. "Can I come in?"

"Sure," I said, stepping back. He walked into the room, and I closed the door behind him.

This was the Ramón I liked so much. His face relaxed and open. That twisting tooth in his smile.

"I brought you something," he said, and he held out his hand. In it was a drawing like the one he'd made of me in the pizza place. But in this one, I was wearing the Arantxa costume, I had my natural hair texture, and behind me was the word "RAZA" in big graffiti letters.

"Mexican and Puerto Rican, huh?" he said. "I think I owe you an apology. You don't seem ashamed to be Latina, at all."

"So you saw the—ah—clips on social media?" I asked.

"My favorite is that original meme: 'I'm Latina, you pendejo!'"

I shook my head, mortified.

"But there's more to it," he said, scrutinizing me.

"What do you mean?" I asked.

"You're some kind of . . . I don't know," he said. "You show up here at the most random time of year. Asking all these questions. You end up stopping some crazy white supremacist who stole Kyle's dad's identity. What are you? Some kind of teenage cop?"

"What?" I asked, hoping I wouldn't blush. Don't blush. Do NOT blush. "I'm *not* a cop."

"Not police?" he asked. "So . . . FBI?"

"I'm not affiliated with the government," I said.

"Then, what?" he said. "You're part of some vigilante group?"

"That's crazy," I said. "Can't a girl have a heroic moment? If I were a boy, would you assume I was part of something bigger?"

"Yes," he said. "I would have the exact same questions. Like, it's pretty suspicious that you're going back to Los Angeles now, after you've eliminated the threat."

"It's just that my stepdad saw me on TV," I said. "And he and my mom got to talking, and they're gonna try to work it out."

"Sounds like a cover story," he said.

"Will you come visit me in LA?" I asked.

"Will you come visit me?" he asked.

"I thought it might make more sense for you to visit me, so you could look at colleges," I said.

"What?" he asked.

"You said you were thinking about going to college," I said. "Why not college in LA? There are a ton of schools. I'll be going to one of them eventually."

"I'll think about it," he said.

"Meanwhile, LA is just a bus ride away from here," I said.

"I'll think about it very strongly."

"I'll take that as a yes," I said.

"Yes," he said.

I leaned in and kissed him, and he kissed back. It was different this time. My heart, my whole body was light. The assignment was over, and I could be myself.

"And just think," I said. "This time there are no racist white guys to break us apart."

"No," he said. "Thanks to you eliminating the threat."

We kissed again.

"I just have one more question," he said.

"Uh-oh," I said.

"How come you let me call you by the wrong name this whole time?" he asked.

I shrugged.

And then he said it. My name. In my language. "Andréa."

Later, before he went home, I asked him one final question.

"Now that you know a little more about me, does that boyfriend offer still stand?"

His eyes widened. "Of course," he said. "I didn't know if you could forgive me."

"Maybe I just defeated a white supremacist to prove my Latinidad to you," I said.

"Ha ha," he said. "Fat chance."

"I know, right," I said. "But it would be the ultimate romantic gesture."

"Like for an anniversary," he said. "Stopping white extremist terrorism is always a tasteful gift."

We kissed again.

"I should've had more faith in you," he said when we came up for air. "If I did, I would have been able to see you live in action."

"Speaking of anniversaries," I said. "We could go to next year's ComxCon together. If we practice, maybe we can even enter the Triángulo tournament."

"It's a date," he said.

Our flight had scarcely taken off when Mom passed out in the aisle seat. We had the row to ourselves and had put up all the armrests. I scooted over to the window seat and watched Arizona get smaller and smaller.

I couldn't wait to see Papi and Carlos again. Now that my brother was ten, Mom said I could let him borrow the Triángulo comics. She said she would let me take him to see the movie in the theaters when it came out.

Since my cover had been blown, I would be able to say much more than usual about the operation. But some parts nobody in my family needed to know, like the fact that I had my first boyfriend and my first kiss.

I scrolled through my phone to the photo of the four of us: me, Ramón, Imani, and Kyle. I realized it wasn't just the firsts with Ramón. It was the firsts with Imani, too. I'd had my first best friend as a teenager.

I was still going to be working actively with the Factory, even though my name and face were out there and I probably wouldn't be able to be the lead agent on an undercover assignment anymore. But I had no idea when Imani and I would be able to cross paths again.

Impulsively—while Mom was asleep—I transferred Imani's number from my assignment phone into my real phone.

It was a short flight to LA, and I'd text Imani the minute we landed. I'd keep it simple. Something like "Just landed at LAX. Preparing to brave LA traffic."

And then a GIF of Arantxa flying. But I would send it from my real phone.

Imani was a spy. And a teenager. I trusted that she would be able to decode what the message really meant: "I miss you already. You can reach me at this number. Friends like you don't come along every day. I'm never gonna let you go."

AUTHOR'S NOTE

My mother, with her light olive skin, straight sandy hair, and green eyes, is often mistaken for a white woman. Her Puerto Rican mother *never* was—my abuela had dark olive skin, dark hair, and a thick accent. And when my mother was in her twenties, she had a Black boyfriend and later a Black husband, with whom she had a Black daughter—me. Perhaps there were a few years when my mother moved in the world alone and was seen as a white woman. But nearly all of her life has been impacted by the vulnerability to racism that targeted other members of her family. And beyond that—however anyone may see her—she still carries the ancestral memory of racism in her lineage: generations of terror, grief, and rage from genocide, slavery, and colonization. My mother once told me that the worst part of being mistaken for white was hearing what white people said about people of color when they thought we weren't listening. I suppose that was when I first began to imagine my mother—a young Latina being perceived as white—as a spy.

My parents divorced when I was three. My father is African American from South Carolina and West Indian from St. Kitts and Nevis. Throughout the Americas, under conditions of slavery and colonization, African, Indigenous, and European people mixed in a spectrum of shades and hair textures, while those in power imposed a racial hierarchy with whiteness consistently on top. In the United States, during the period of enslavement, race was defined in a Black/white binary, with a "one-drop rule" that meant that if a person had any African heritage—however distant—they were legally defined as Black and could be held in the condition of slavery. Race worked differently in Latin America; it was less of a binary, and under certain conditions, many generations of whitening could lead to white status. Colorism in our Black and Latine communities has meant consistent favoritism of and better outcomes for individuals and groups that resemble white people. Racism has slightly different flavors in different parts of the Americas, but in societies built on white supremacy, everyone is encouraged to yearn for whiteness as the ultimate prize.

My mother could have decided to live her life as a white woman, but she chose to be proudly Latina and built a life in solidarity with others in the BIPOC community. Much of her life's work has focused on fighting racism and police violence, mostly as it impacts Black people. And yet I also saw how other people's racial confusion about her sometimes left her isolated or cut off from community.

In contrast, some folks on her side of the family made very conscious choices to hide their heritage. While that choice often allows a passing person to prosper economically, living that lie can carry high mental and emotional costs. I think of one family member who struggled deeply with this issue and died young.

But many Latine people don't seem particularly tormented by this approach. There are plenty of folks in our community who choose to pass for white, to assimilate, to collude with colorism and favor the whiteness in our community, or to live lives that uphold white supremacy. I chose to write this book in praise of the solidarity and connection between the broader BIPOC community and light-skinned Latine folks like my mother who never forget who their family is and are ready to throw down for all of us against racism with everything they've got.

And while I hope that *Undercover Latina* will resonate with readers of all backgrounds and skin tones, I believe that the book offers a particular invitation for anyone who has that proximity to whiteness: an invitation to examine and wrestle with these issues. People need opportunities to debrief on the light-skinned experience of racism and to face the difficulty of staying connected with your community when white supremacy favors you over your family and your people and is constantly trying to separate you. People need to heal from the trauma of being mis-identified, of being presumed not to belong to your gente, along with the confusion of being offered privileges in exchange for denying parts of yourself. The guilt or shame you might feel if you accept those privileges. The frustration you might feel if you reject the privileges but people in your community still find you suspect. Unfortunately, many of the spaces where we can confront these issues haven't been built yet, and if you try to talk about this in broader conversations among people of color, you may be misunderstood. It can be hard for people who have been denied these privileges and are constantly targeted with racism to empathize with those who live in the shadow side of access. But part of the battle for justice involves building more spaces for healing and adding these stories to the never-ending list of reasons we need to eliminate racism.

This battle requires all of us as people of color to explore the different ways we've chosen to collaborate with white supremacy or to stand in solidarity with our communities. This is a call for anyone who has lost their way. Whatever jokes you've laughed along with, whoever you may have thrown under the bus for mainstream approval, whatever parts of yourselves you've straightened or lightened or hidden or lied about, you are still one of us. You belong with us. You are a part of us. Whatever your journey has been up till now, healing can be found. It's worth it to struggle to find your place in the community.

In the movement. Within your lineage. Within yourself. It's not always easy. But the battle to end racism needs all of us. Your community needs you to stand firm against rising white nationalism in all its disguises. Let this book be an invitation for all of us to come home to the fight for justice—together.

ACKNOWLEDGMENTS

I grew up in Northern California on land stolen from Mexico by the United States and originally stolen from the Ohlone people. As an AfroLatina who grew up in a community where the vast majority of Spanish speakers were Mexican American, I have often felt like an undercover Latina myself. In addition to thanking my literary team—my fabulous editor, Andrea Tompa, and my spectacular agent, Jenni Ferrari-Adler—I want to thank all the gente who have contributed to this book both knowingly and unknowingly and helped me find myself and all my stories: the West Coast Chicanx OG homies, Lea Arellano and Marcos Tapia; the Boricua crew for all times, Aurora Levins-Morales, Yara and Leyka Alma-Bonilla, Yulahlia Hernández, and especially Alicia Raquel, who had brilliant replies to a million "what do you think of this?" texts; the beloved wife-and-wife writer team Carolina DeRobertis and Pam Harris; and Sofia Quintero, Aida Salazar, and Angie Cruz, for game-changing support. Big love to all the teachers, youth workers, and fam who did childcare so I could write, especially Coco, Stuart, Larry, Paci, Neens, Kris, Quetzal, Emily, and the Monarchs. Plus, special shout-out to Dee for listening to the book not once but *twice* and for giving amazing feedback. Finally, thanks to Ally Carter and Robin Benway for the YA spy girl books that inspired me. It's a delight to follow in your footsteps. ¡Gracias!